THE HAUNTED

by

Jonas Saul

PUBLISHED BY:
Imagine Press Inc.
Ebook ISBN: 978-1-927404-37-9
Paperback ISBN: 978-1-998047-11-6
Hardcover ISBN: 978-1-998047-12-3

The Haunted
Copyright © 2014 by Jonas Saul

The Decoy (Thirty-Three)
The Disappearance (Thirty-Four)
The Whole Truth (Thirty-Five)
Alex (Thirty-Six)
Parkman (Thirty-Seven)
Darwin (Thirty-Eight)
Aaron (Thirty-Nine)
Remains To Be Seen (Forty)

The Jake Wood Novels

The Immortal Gene (Book One)
The Immortal Target (Book Two)

Standalone Novels

'Til Death Do Us Part
The Drowning
The Woman in the Woods
The Threat
The Specter
The Mafia Trilogy
A Murder in Time
Frequency of the Dead

Co-Authored Novels

Collision Course (Written with Gary Ponzo)
There Will Be Blood (Written with Rania Stone)
The Soulless (Written with Rania Stone)

Short Story Collections

Twisted Fate (Tales of Horror)

Twists of Fate (Tales of Hope)

Chapter 1

THE HEAVY RAIN BROKE through the violence, the screaming. As Vivian's consciousness wavered and her eyes rolled back in her head, his fist connected with her cheekbone. With that last hammering crunch, he mercifully ended the pain, the horror, the terror.

But it was the rain that snapped Sarah back to the present. She sat up straighter in the car, her face wet. She wiped her eyes and dabbed at the sweat from her brow, for a brief moment wondering if the roof of the car had leaked.

"You fell asleep," Aaron said.

He was leaning forward at the steering wheel, his hands at ten and two as he guided the vehicle through the deluge that woke Sarah from another one of Vivian's nightmares. The rain pounded the windshield, the wipers unable to keep up.

After a moment, breathing regularly again, calmer, Sarah

said, "We should pull over somewhere. This rain is crazy."

"We're almost there. Maybe five minutes left."

"You really want to go out in this?"

He snuck a glance at her, then back at the road. "You slept for a bit. I didn't want to wake you."

She looked out the window, then up at the sky. Lighter clouds moved just ahead, the dark, black clouds easing aside. Maybe the rain would subside after all.

"You were dreaming," Aaron said. "You okay?"

"Just fine."

"Cold sweats, rapid breathing, high blood pressure, no doubt, and tears when you wake up usually mean fine," he said. "I should know that by now. Because fine stands for Fucked Interior, Nice Exterior."

She stretched out her feet, ignoring his taunt. They'd been in the car for hours now. Coffee was on her mind. Not Vivian anymore.

"I'll talk about it, but not now. Seeing what happened to my sister vividly in my mind, like I was there, living it, then waking to talk about it, isn't going to work for me. Wait until I'm having a good day. Then we'll sit with a glass of wine and discuss everything."

"You never have a good day."

She shot him a look. More of a warning.

"I'm not being pessimistic," he said. "Just realistic. Since you helped Detective Hirst in Los Angeles, you've been taking it easy. No more fighting bad guys. I know. I get it. A much-deserved break. Your foot healed nicely, and you've been working out and training for over six months. You're healed and ready for whatever comes in the future." He slowed the car and pulled to the shoulder. "But there isn't a day that goes by without one or more Vivian memories." The car stopped. He took her hand. She didn't pull it away. "I'm worried about you. I mean, how much of her do you take on? And how much do you lose of yourself?"

Sarah felt another tear threaten to drop and hated the weakness. She had gotten closer to Aaron. Their relationship had deepened, partly because she hadn't been actively pursuing murderers and rapists, which was Aaron's preference, and partly because she discovered she really needed him. For the first time in her life, she needed something, and that something was Aaron. He was strong when she was weak, right when she was wrong. He was the man to her woman, the yin to her yang. In the recent break she had taken to heal her foot, as her consciousness merged with Vivian's, her heart had started to merge with Aaron's.

Relationships are supposed to be mysterious, intriguing, and fun.

Only Sarah wasn't ready for mystery or intrigue. She wanted solid facts and grounded details. She was an intellectual who came from a place of logic. Decisions were routinely logic based. Aaron, her first real, long-term relationship, was sitting in the car's driver's seat, and there were times—many times—when she had no idea what to do or say, which felt like a weakness to her.

"I'm not losing myself," she said. "I'm still here."

He looked away. The car continued to idle. A large truck drove by, water splashing up along Aaron's side of the car. Then he turned back to her.

Before he could speak, she said, "Let's get this over with."

He let go of her hand and pulled the car back onto the

road. Minutes later, the rain eased off as Aaron descended a side road leading to the cemetery.

Sarah shuddered, a shiver running through her as the headstones came into view. One of them belonged to her sister, Vivian. She rubbed her clammy hands back and forth across her thighs.

"You okay?" Aaron asked. "You sure you're ready to do this?"

She didn't respond. When the car stopped by the mausoleum, Sarah got out and stood in the rain that had subsided to a soft drizzle. She didn't need to consult the gravesite directions in her back pocket. She'd memorized them two days ago.

Vivian was buried in two green-grass sections south of the mausoleum. Her headstone wasn't the kind that stood up. It lay flat, surrounded by others like it.

Sarah wiped her face, flung her hair over her shoulders, and walked. Aaron stayed close but not close enough to invade her space. She was here to pay her respects, to visit the earthly spot where Vivian's body rested in peace.

Her lips formed a half smile at the thought of Vivian resting peacefully. There was no peace with Vivian or anyone involved with her. Sarah knew this first hand.

Mentally, the closer Vivian and Sarah got, the more memories filtered through. Sarah could discern two childhood memories now, some distant, some near, but only one version of the childhood memories was hers. Like when Vivian burned herself on their mother's curling iron after being told not to touch it. Or Vivian's first bike at the age of three. Sarah had to wait until she was six to learn how to ride a bike, but by the time she was eight and had a new babysitter, the cop who lived next door, she no longer took an interest in her bike.

But along with the nostalgic memories came the scary ones, the terrible ones, the nightmares of Vivian's last hour on earth. For some reason, those memories were the most vivid; the ones planted the deepest.

Sarah was trying to live with those memories or at least cope with them. Maybe they would fade in time. Maybe she would even begin to forget them in years to come. But right now, Vivian's memories haunted her.

Enough that she had recently decided to meet with a psychiatrist to help her deal with the unwanted images.

She paused on the wet grass, her running shoes sinking slightly, the ground still soggy from winter, the warmth of summer still a month or two away. April was the first full month of spring, of things reborn, life anew. It was also Sarah's birthday. Today, April 22, Sarah turned twenty-six years old and never paid her respects at her sister's grave. She had asked Aaron to take the drive with her. He would return to Toronto soon, and she wouldn't see him until June.

The headstones close to her read of early deaths and teenage deaths but also of people who lived into their eighties and were buried with mom, dad, sister, and brother. A few of the headstones were relatively small, with just MOM or DAD written on them. Others had entire sentences, life achievements etched into their granite or marble surfaces.

In the distance, two dark mounds depicted sites of recent burials.

Aaron stepped closer. He touched her arms gently. "Found her?" he asked in a whisper.

She shook her head and reached for the instructions in

her pocket.

A car entered the cemetery. The dark-colored vehicle turned in and angled away from them, following the concrete drive to another grave, another lost loved one.

The rain had stopped completely now, and the sun peeked out through a distant gathering of clouds. Still, Sarah shivered. She had never done anything like this in her life. She had been around death and caused quite a few, but cemeteries were new.

With the paper in hand, still folded, she turned and looked into Aaron's eyes. She saw his yearning, his longing to be there for her, protect her. It was what she loved and hated about him at the same time.

They embraced. She held him tight while holding back the tears, the wave of emotion. She had gotten to know Vivian in an entirely different way over the past year. It was almost as if they had lived their lives together, and now Vivian was gone, buried.

But Vivian hadn't gone anywhere. Even though her body rotted underfoot, she was very much alive and rooted inside Sarah's psyche.

As Sarah pulled away from Aaron, Vivian's voice echoed in her head.

"To the left ..."

Sarah headed that way, the paper with the instructions crumpled in her palm.

"Slightly to the right now ..."

She hopped between two stones, the ground soft, yielding. The sun reached her now, warming her skin and offering comfort.

"There ..."

Sarah stopped. She slid the paper back into her pocket. An image of Vivian running out into the sun in the backyard of their house with the garden hose in her hand flitted through Sarah's mind. Summertime. The sprinkler. Running back and forth under the water. Laughter.

Sarah looked down at the stone that marked her sister's grave and let the flood of tears go. She wept for Vivian and the times they would never have together.

The epitaph read *Life Goes On*.

"This is meant to be," Vivian whispered in Sarah's inner ear. "So we could do what we do."

"Nooo," Sarah said under her breath.

She dropped to her knees, the wet ground soaking through her jeans instantly.

"No." Louder this time.

She had forgotten the flowers in the back seat.

Without looking up, she said, "Aaron, could you go and get the—"

The bouquet of lilies materialized beside her. "Brought them with us," he said.

She hadn't seen him grab them. But she hadn't been paying too much attention.

She took the flowers and gently laid them alongside the name Vivian Roberts.

Another memory surfaced. One of Vivian's last moments, her last breath. The pain in her face, her chest as her heart struggled to beat and her lungs screamed for air. The pain in her groin as she struggled uselessly against her murderer, her rapist.

Sarah yelped, dropped her hands to the grass, and balled them into fists, ripping grass out by the roots and clumping it in her palm. She ground her teeth together and seethed silently at the injustice of it all. It was one thing to know what happened, to lose a loved one, and to keep moving forward. But to have to feel, to almost endure what they endured, was something else entirely.

How much of her sanity was compromised by these images? Could she continue what she had been doing for the past seven-plus years with a traitor for a mind? Before she was shot in the head in Toronto last year, Vivian couldn't get in at this level. Now Vivian was another consciousness, another being inside Sarah. One that could even control Sarah's body whether Sarah allowed it or not.

Until recently, her sister had only entered her sparingly and with massive effort, but now Vivian had made a home inside Sarah's consciousness. In some respects, Sarah welcomed it because Vivian could just talk now. No more notes, no more pens, and papers. But with that came all of Vivian. Even her darkest moments.

Aaron's hands found Sarah's shoulders. She shirked him off. This was between the sisters.

Sarah lowered to her elbows, breathed in the wet soil smell, and tried to get herself under control.

"I'm sorry," Vivian whispered in her head. "There are thoughts I can't control. But you need to leave now."

Sarah's head snapped up. She wiped her eyes with the backs of her wrists and scanned the immediate area, instantly alert. She hadn't brought any weapons with her. The gun was back at the cabin she had rented until June.

Am I being paranoid?

"What's happening?" she asked. "Why do we have to leave?"

"Just go," Vivian whispered. The lightness of Vivian's voice floated in her mind like feathers could talk. "Meet with your doctor. He'll help. Then we have something to do. Something important."

"Why won't you tell me where that cop is? My old babysitter?"

Whenever Aaron saw Sarah talking to herself, he backed away to give her privacy. He understood who she was talking to, but she suspected it freaked him out.

"All in good time ..."

Vivian's voice trailed off. A feeling of retreat, a withdrawal, whooshed through her. Sarah was alone with Aaron. The feeling was absolute. She took another moment to collect herself, then got to her feet and brushed the dirt from her knees.

Aaron waited patiently five headstones away. He offered a gentle smile. She nodded that she was okay, then scanned the grounds again.

The vehicle that had entered the cemetery moments before looked like a Ford Fusion. It was parked by one of the fresh mounds of dirt. Two men in black leather coats stood by the mound, heads bowed. The one who faced her seemed to be watching them. Even though his head was aimed downward, she felt his eyes on her. But how was that possible? No one knew where they were going today, and even if someone knew, why follow her?

She blinked hard, wiped her eyes, and stared at the men.

They turned from the mound and headed for their vehicle.

"Did you see those two?" she asked.

"Yeah? What about them?"

"Were they watching us?"

After a moment, Aaron said, "Not that I could tell."

The car eased down the narrow road meandering through the plots.

With one last look at Vivian's burial site, Sarah blew a kiss and turned away. She linked her arm with Aaron's as they headed for the car.

Once on the concrete, Sarah stomped her feet to remove the residue from the wet grass. In a harsh suddenness, their car alarm sounded.

Her head snapped up. No one was near the car as the alarm blared. Aaron fumbled for the key fob in his pocket, brought it out, and silenced the alarm.

"How did that happen?" he asked.

"You didn't bump the panic button on the fob by accident, did you?"

He shook his head and stared down at the keys. "They were in my pocket. My arm was in yours until we stepped onto this little road."

Sarah deepened her voice and tried to emulate Vincent Price. "Maybe it was Vivian or some other ghost wanting to make contact."

"Don't be weird."

"What's weird? My voice or the alarm?"

"Both."

She smacked his arm before he could block it or step back. "Let's go. I need to get back to the cabin."

As they drove the winding lane toward the exit, Aaron said, "I'm going to miss you."

"It's only been two weeks. In six weeks, I'll come home. Then maybe I'll visit you in Toronto."

"Overall, it's two months. That's a lot."

She opened the car window for fresh air to replace the humid and thick air after the rain. "It may be a lot, but it's needed."

"Isn't there someone you can see near Santa Rosa?"

"I don't want to bump into my doctor, the man who knows what's inside my head while buying oranges or bread at the local grocery store. I rented this cabin for two months and set up six appointments with a psychiatrist with a purpose."

"I know, you told me. Sartre said something like, 'If you're lonely when you're alone, then you're in bad company.'"

"That's exactly why I need to spend two months alone."

"But you're seeing a doctor weekly."

"Aaron. You know what I mean."

He pulled out of the cemetery and headed back the way they had come, a smile playing across his lips. "I know, but I can't be faulted for trying. I've been missing you, and I'm going to miss you. Parkman's missing you. Your parents are —"

"Really? Add all the pressure you want. I'll make it three months. Maybe four. The cabin's a month-to-month lease. I've retained the first option. But no problem, just keep pushing."

He nodded, that smile still there. When he reached for the radio, Sarah looked forward and saw the Ford Fusion from the cemetery again.

It was coming toward them.

The same one?

Before it passed, she visually confirmed it was the same

men from the cemetery. Both wore their leather jackets. Both had close-cropped hair, military-like.

And both men stared at her with a look she had seen on men's faces many times.

Hatred.

Chapter 2

As the sun descended behind a curtain of swollen and bruised purplish clouds, Sarah retreated inside the cabin, locking the door behind her. It was quite similar to the cabin Gert had taken her when she was eighteen. Over the past few years, she had written her life story in a series of books so that one day, when she was gone, she could share what she had done with whoever cared to read it. Recently there had been more time for writing. She had been making notes on her time in Italy, Kelowna, Canada, and Los Angeles. Soon, after locating her old babysitter, she would write the first drafts of those memoirs.

Her glass was refilled with red wine, and Blue October played on the iPad speaker on the bookshelf. She fired up her MacBook Pro and continued her search for Cole Lincoln, her old babysitter.

She had discovered he no longer worked for any police

organization. Without the proper hacker skills required, getting into the DMV website or searching city records for his name was out of the question. Google was the only tool in her arsenal, but nothing useful came up. As far as she could tell, he did not maintain a Facebook account, Twitter, or Instagram. After leaving the police force for undisclosed reasons, Lincoln just disappeared.

Even Vivian was strangely silent on the matter.

Thinking of her sister, Sarah leaned back in her chair and took another sip of her wine. After leaving the gravesite earlier, she gave Aaron credit for not prying, not asking what Vivian had talked to her about. She thought back to the men in the cemetery, the ones they passed on the road, and realized her paranoia had gotten the better of her. Would she have stared at them as intensely if Vivian hadn't asked her to leave the cemetery? If she hadn't stared at them in such a way, maybe they wouldn't have noticed her.

There was nothing else in her life happening. No criminals on her radar. No detectives looking for help, and nothing from Vivian. Nothing except routine check-ins like earlier at the cemetery.

And now Aaron was gone for another week, only to return with groceries and supplies before he left for Toronto for a few months. He would stay the night and leave in the morning. Even though he was to head to Toronto after that, she was strangely happy. In her life, the kind of peace and quiet the cabin offered had been rare.

Blue October sang about being foiled while she closed her eyes, swished the wine around in her mouth, and listened for her sister on the inside. She could usually detect her lingering, rummaging around.

Since leaving the cemetery, the devastating Vivian memories had eased off. Maybe that signaled the end of them. If so, she wouldn't need any help in maintaining her sanity. Maybe she would tell Dr. Williams she might not come again after their first meeting.

Sarah jumped at a soft rapping like something bumped the outer wall on the south-facing side of the cabin. A branch snapped and swung in front of the window. She looked in time to see it swing back and forth until it stopped.

She set her wine glass on the table in one fluid motion and pushed her chair back. In sock feet, she rushed for the dark bedroom, retrieved her Glock from the back of the night table, and huddled by the bedroom window, her eyes closed to adjust to the darkness faster.

The half-moon wasn't bright enough to illuminate the area outside the window. Tiny bushes and shrubs surrounded the cabin. A row of tall deciduous trees lined the back about ten yards away, near the edge of the property. As far as she could tell, nothing moved out there.

And nothing moved on the inside, either.

"Vivian, where are you?" she whispered. "You wanna tell me what that was? Or who that was?"

When Vivian remained silent, Sarah moved through the cabin killing the lights as she went. At the door, the only door in the two-room building, she wrapped her finger around the trigger guard of the Glock and eased the door open. Her stomach fluttered, and it made her crack a smile. She hadn't been in any kind of action or danger in so many months it almost felt new again. It was something that lifted her spirits and propelled her adrenaline. Others jumped from planes for the rush. Sarah needed the cloak and dagger of the chase, the hunt, and the fight.

Her head low, she slipped outside and put her back to the wall beside the door. Then she scanned the area immediately around her, the Glock following her gaze like a first-person-shooter video game—which had been part of her recent training, using a game as a simulator.

The landscape was void of humans, and the air was completely still.

Then what the hell made that noise? What moved the branch?

With the cabin at her back, she moved away from the moonlight to remain in the darkest regions of the property. After a dozen steps along the side, the sound of twigs snapping underfoot held her up short.

She stopped, listened, held her breath, and waited.

Slowly, her weapon leading the way, she eased around the corner.

A white-tailed doe chewed on a rose bush at the back of the cabin. Alert to her presence now, the deer's head snapped up and looked toward her, then trotted away and disappeared into the brush and trees.

"Shit. Pulled away from my research and wine by a hungry animal."

After another scan of the property line, which was easier to see now that her eyes were fully adjusted to the dark, Sarah headed back inside.

She closed and locked the cabin door, flicked on the lights, and replaced the Glock in its holder behind the night table.

It wasn't another hour before she had finished the wine, exhausted Google in search of Lincoln, until she finally found the email of Lincoln's sister, who now lived in Atlanta. She emailed Rebecca Lincoln with a false story about being an old friend. She was trying to find Rebecca's brother, Cole, without much success. Could Rebecca offer any advice as to where Cole might be?

It didn't bother Sarah in the least to lie to Rebecca in her missive or to involve the sister in locating Cole. He had to pay for what he did to her all those years ago. It was the right thing to do. Even Vivian agreed. How many other victims had Lincoln abused since having gotten away with it? Although it would be nice if Vivian would just tell her where Cole was so she could stop wasting time.

She prepared for bed, set the cabin's alarm, and brought her iPad into the bedroom. Within minutes of hitting the pillow, she was asleep.

After a shower, breakfast, and getting dressed in the morning, she turned the alarm off to leave the cabin, reset it, and stepped outside. In the light of the sunny morning, she noticed large footprints in the dirt. The prints were not hers. It was a man's print, at least twelve inches long. Yesterday's rain had left the ground soft and now revealed the footprints of her late-night visitors.

So someone had been here last night.

She closed the cabin door behind her, locked it, and followed the footprints. They circled the cabin, approaching the window where the branch had been disturbed.

Aaron hadn't gotten out of his car when he dropped her off after the cemetery visit yesterday. The prints were too big to be his anyway. There had been no visitors since she moved in for her two-month stint. These particular footprints were new and meant only one thing.

Someone was keeping tabs on her.

But who? And why?

Could Lincoln know she's looking for him? Could he have someone watching her, and that's why Vivian said it would happen in its own time? Were those two men in the Ford Fusion from yesterday Lincoln's men?

If so, was Aaron being watched, too?

She pulled her iPhone out to check the time. Another hour until her first appointment with Dr. Williams. She would still make it on time, but on the way, she would call Aaron and warn him to watch his back.

She had left the Glock in the cabin but wouldn't need it for a doctor's appointment. Once in the car, she headed out to the main road.

Until whoever was on her tail confronted her or she discovered them back tonight, she would carry on as normally as possible.

When do I ever let an asshole change my schedule for me?

But when she nabbed them, she would definitely change their schedule.

Among other things.

Chapter 3

SARAH PULLED INTO AN empty spot near the front doors to the little clinic where Dr. Williams had an office. During the forty-minute ride over, she watched the rearview mirror repeatedly in search of a tail and was disappointed to find none. Unless they were exceptional at what they did and could stay undetected as they followed her, she was confident she rode in alone.

During the drive, she tried Aaron on his cell phone three times but kept getting his machine. On the third call, she left him a brief message explaining what she found outside the cabin. Whoever was tracking her might be following him as well. Before she hung up, she mentioned that Vivian had nothing to say and that he would be the first she called as soon as she did.

She exited the car, already missing her motorcycle. She'd bought a Dodge Charger because she didn't want to ride the bike during the previous winter. There was still a healthy financial nest egg from when her parents sold their house and moved to Santa Rosa, not to mention the money Oliver Payne offered her after his wife was killed behind Sarah's parents' house a while back.

The front of the doctor's building offered manicured bushes, clean windows, and little signage. The bottom floor housed a lawyer's office, with Dr. Williams's office upstairs.

She entered the front doors and pushed the buzzer by Williams's name. The inside doors buzzed open.

The stairs were off to the left beside an elevator. She chose the stairs, but before heading up, she took one more look behind her through the doors to the outside. Then she flipped her cell to vibrate, took a deep breath, and started up the steps.

A Joe Girard quote flitted through her head: *The elevator to success is broken. You will have to take the stairs one step at a time.*

She was doing that by meeting with a specialist that would hopefully help her cope with Vivian's thoughts. This guy came recommended. Vivian herself had supplied his name and number. Said he was an expert in past-life regression and had worked for years with bipolar patients and schizoaffective disorders. He even helped out at the Amy Greg Psychiatric Hospital.

At first, Sarah had been put off.

"I'm not fucking crazy," she had railed at her sister.

But what Vivian had explained was not so much Dr. Williams's specialty but that he was adept at dealing with two personalities in one mind. Since Sarah was completely sane but now living with Vivian's presence in her mind, he was the best doctor to help Sarah deal with it.

She planned to meet him, interview him, and then tell the doctor what was on her mind if she approved of him because he was bound to confidentiality. This process wouldn't have much chance of success without the truth. Dr. Williams needed to know exactly what he was dealing with.

Nervousness crept in as she neared the second floor. Her insides fluttered. She stopped and placed a hand on her stomach.

What's this all about?

She was rarely nervous. Was it because she couldn't get a hold of Aaron? Could something have happened to him? Talking to a doctor couldn't be it. She'd walk out in a heartbeat if she didn't like him.

Or could Vivian be nervous for her? That was something she hadn't considered before. How far in had Vivian ensconced herself? If this was Vivian's nervousness, what else would Sarah feel in the coming days, weeks, or years? Could she handle the intrusion long-term?

Without further delay, she opened the door on the second floor. The area had a new construction smell to it. The baseboards had tape on them, and the paint was still drying.

She opened Suite 201's door and stepped into an empty waiting room. There were three chairs, a circular table with magazines on it—*Psychology Today*, *Scientific American Mind*, and *National Geographic*—and a water cooler.

Behind the small admittance window, a woman wrote something down.

Sarah cleared her throat. The woman looked up.

"Can I help you?" she asked.

"I have an appointment with Dr. Williams."

The woman flipped through a few pages in a large book, smiled, and nodded.

"Your name?" she asked.

"Sarah Roberts."

"Right. He'll see you now." She pointed to Sarah's right. "Enter through that door. It'll take you into his office."

"He knows I'm here? He's expecting me right now?"

The woman frowned. "You have an appointment."

"That's not what I mean. You haven't paged or called him. He has no idea I'm even in the building, yet I'm to walk right into his office."

"You're his only client today," the woman said, hesitating like talking to a child. "After you, he's on holiday for the rest of the week."

Sarah started for the door. Something might be wrong here. The new office was on a recently built or renovated floor. Renowned doctor but far from any major city. Odd secretary. A waiting room that appeared to be unused. However, that could be because the move to this building was so recent. Or this could all just be the last seven years of fighting for her life, being stabbed and shot and killing people along the way, working itself up into paranoia that she's unfamiliar with during a break like the kind she recently had.

Something more for the doctor to deal with.

Inside the office was the proverbial couch with a comfortable armchair beside it. On the opposite wall sat two leather armchairs. Sarah took the one that looked out onto the parking lot below so she could keep an eye on her car.

She only had to wait a few minutes before Dr. Williams opened a door behind the large banker's desk and entered the office. The quick glimpse Sarah got of the room beyond was of another unfinished room with no paint and no carpeting.

She got to her feet and extended her hand. "Dr. Williams?"

"Sarah?" He shook her proffered hand. "Or would you prefer I call you Miss Roberts?"

"Sarah's fine."

She retook her seat by the window, stealing a glance outside.

"Can you tell me a little about yourself and what brought you here today?" he asked.

Sarah cleared her throat. "Maybe this was a mistake."

"How so?"

"I don't have an issue or a mental problem."

"Many of the people I see don't either."

That took her by surprise. She paused, leaned back in her chair, and assessed him. He had a thick mustache that connected to an even thicker beard. Bushy eyebrows. The whites of his eyes were clean, lacking redness. His shirt was pressed, his pants tailored. He took his role seriously. There was intelligence in his eyes.

"Enjoying the new office?" Sarah asked.

He looked around, then back at her. "Yes. But the renovations aren't what you came to talk to me about, are they?"

"No, they aren't."

She stared at him a moment longer, contemplating the next question, how to word it. She wanted to interview him and see that he was a good fit for her, but she was afraid she wouldn't be able to get past her trust issues. For years she had learned that the only one she could trust and rely on was herself and sometimes Parkman. What made her think she could meet this total stranger and, by virtue of his position, tell him what was going on with Vivian inside her head? The haunted nights, the dark dreams, her own thoughts shaken by the turbulence of Vivian's thoughts.

"Then let me start with a few innocuous questions," Williams said. "Would you be willing to answer them? They are the kind that break the ice. Once that's done, you could decide to continue or cancel this meeting. There'll be no fee if you cancel in ten minutes when I finish my questions. Would that suffice?"

Sarah nodded. "Sounds fair. Shoot."

"I want you to imagine a vast desert, sand blowing here and there. In this desert sits a cube. In your mind, what does this cube look like? What's it made of? How strong is it? Or how weak? Tell me everything you can about the cube."

Chapter 4

"Parkman, I know what you're saying, and I trust her, but something doesn't feel right about this."

"Aaron, there's one thing you have to learn about Sarah. She's a survivor. And she's got Vivian. Nothing's going to happen to her."

"I know she's a survivor, Parkman."

"That means that whatever is going on, she either already knows about it, will know about it soon, or nothing is going on."

"She's been researching that ex-babysitter of hers. A man named Cole Lincoln."

"I'm aware of that."

"Did you find anything on him?"

"She didn't ask me to look. I don't pry when it comes to Sarah. If she needs me, I'm there. Otherwise, she'll handle this herself. You have to remember, Aaron, I love her, too.

Just in a different way."

"Yeah, okay, but I feel something's wrong."

"You want my advice?" Parkman asked.

Aaron waited a heartbeat before answering. He knew what the advice would be and didn't want to hear it.

"Sure," he said, dejected. "Go ahead."

"Leave her alone in that cabin for the two months. Go back to Toronto as you planned. Let her work out whatever she needed to work out with Vivian. Tend to your dojo. Read a book. Watch a movie. Stay busy. Sarah always has a process. This is it. Try anything other than that, and it'll hurt you."

"Got it."

"I'm serious."

"I know."

They hung up, but Aaron felt more unsettled than before the call. How could he have thought Parkman would agree with him?

After grabbing his overnight bag, he exited the motel and headed for the front desk to return the key. He'd be back, but next week he'd stay at the cabin with Sarah for the night. That was her promise to him. Until her first meeting with Dr. Williams, she wanted solitude, minus yesterday's cemetery visit.

Parkman could love her any way he wanted, but Aaron didn't have to leave her alone in a cabin suffering from the dreams, the mental hauntings, as Sarah put it.

Something has to be done.

But what? How far was he willing to go? And how much would that push Sarah away?

He dropped the key off to the clerk, told her his room

number and that he was checking out, and headed for the car. On the way across the parking lot, he decided it might be best to leave Sarah alone. Parkman was right. To have Sarah in your life was to leave her alone.

The car was warm for an April morning, the sun heating it through the windshield. Once inside, the car started, the air on, and he grabbed his cell phone to check his email.

"Missed call …" he muttered to himself.

Sarah.

He dialed her number immediately without listening to the message.

No answer.

He hit the button to listen to the message.

Sarah told him about the visitors she had at the cabin last night.

"Dammit! I knew trouble was brewing."

He squealed out of the parking lot, heading back toward the cabin, a half-hour drive on clear roads.

Then he dialed Parkman back.

"Parkman here."

"It's Aaron."

"I know. Saw the number. What's up?"

"Sarah's in trouble."

Chapter 5

"A CUBE?" SARAH ASKED. "In the desert?"

Dr. Williams nodded, tapping a pen to his lips. "Explain what you see in your mind's eye."

Sarah looked out into the parking lot. The roughly forty parking spaces were pretty empty when she pulled in, but now the lot was barren. Her Charger was parked by the front entrance, only the spoiler on the trunk visible to her.

"I see a decent-sized cube." She met the doctor's eyes. He glanced at his pad of paper and wrote something on it. "It's made of impenetrable steel, but it's relatively light. Strong but light. Like titanium. There are small windows, the kind NASA would use on a spaceship that can withstand immense pressure. Though these windows are hard to see through, so inside the cube remains a mystery. Their only design is to be able to look out from inside the cube. It has stood for a long time without tarnish. The sand does nothing to its exterior. Ultimately, it's immovable."

The doctor held no expression on his face. "Very good. Now tell me, there's a ladder somewhere near the cube. Is the ladder beside it, on it, lying down, or on top of the cube? Where is this ladder, and what's the ladder made of?"

Inside her pocket, her iPhone vibrated.

Probably Aaron.

She would call him back after her appointment.

"The ladder is old. Broken. It can't be used anymore. Not one rung can be trusted. I see the cube in the desert by itself. The ladder is quite a distance away." She paused, steepled her fingers, then said, "This is all very interesting, but what does it have to do with why I'm here?"

He wrote furiously on his notepad. "We'll get to that. I only have a few more questions. When we're done with the questions, I'll share their importance." He returned her gaze. "I won't keep a single detail from you."

"Fair enough."

"Think of a horse. Tell me everything that comes to mind. What kind, what size, what color, and so on."

She mentally pictured the horse and watched him race in the wind.

"A large black stallion. I can see him running in the wind, his long mane flowing out with each strong stroke of his muscular body. The body shines in the sun. I see it clearly. He's gorgeous. Regal. There's one drawback with this one, though."

"What's that?"

"He has a hard time listening. Does what he wants at times. Good horse and all, but I'm never good with someone not listening." She shrugged. "If you're looking for a perfect image, I guess I can't offer one. Even my imaginative horse has drawbacks."

"That's no problem." He wrote more notes.

She glanced outside. At the back of the lot, a dark-colored Ford was parked in a spot half hidden by bushes. She hadn't seen it there before. Nor had she heard a car pull up. The sunlight bounced off the car's hood, making it hard to discern its color.

Is it the same one from yesterday?

"Last two items. Imagine flowers. What kind are they? And where are they in relation to the cube?"

Wanting to finish this, rush it along so she could go check the car outside, she said, "Lilies. There's a graveyard. The flowers are beside a headstone."

It was all she could think of. Yesterday's visit to Vivian's grave. The lilies.

"And finally, a storm," Dr. Williams said. "Tell me where the storm is in relation to the cube. What kind of storm and how intense is it?"

Taking her eyes off the window, she envisioned a storm. "There's a storm over the cube, directly above it. Dark black clouds, lightning. It's always there, never wavering. It rains on and off, and sometimes it pours, but the blackness never leaves. It's what ruined the ladder all these years. But that cube remains untouched."

His eyebrows raised a notch, then settled back down. His nose even flared. He continued to write on his pad.

"Your turn," she said. "What was that all about?"

The Ford was still at the back of the lot. Nothing moved outside. The reflection of the sun still made it too hard to discern the color of the paint. It might be the guys from the cemetery yesterday, or it might not be. Or it might be paranoia. If it was, she was already in the right place.

"Are you prepared for a few revelations?" Williams asked.

"Sure. Hit me with it, Doc." Sarah eased back in the chair and crossed her legs.

This ought to be good.

"The cube represents you and how you view yourself."

"Wow," she said, uncrossing her legs and leaning forward. "That's interesting."

"Yes," Williams glanced at the pad in his lap. "Your self-esteem is represented by the cube size, which you said was *decent-sized*. Impenetrable steel. Light. But strong. You are looking out those NASA windows but not letting people see in too easily. As you age into your mid-twenties, nothing's stopping you or harnessing you, as the sand of the desert did not affect the cube's exterior. The sand is life and how it wears you down. Evidently, you feel the sands of time have given you a free pass for now. I'd be interested in asking you these questions in twenty years' time. I imagine the cube would be vastly different."

"Who knows? You might be surprised by my answer then, too." She leaned back in her chair. "That's quite something. You got all that from the description of a cube?"

"You gave all that to me." He used his finger to find something on the page, then said, "The ladder represents friends in your life. They're broken and can't be trusted, not a single rung, not a single one. The ladder was a distance away, too. That means you don't have a lot of friends."

"I have Aaron and Parkman. That's all I need."

"Who are they?" he asked.

"Aaron's my boyfriend, and Parkman and I work together occasionally. We have for years. Ever since I was twenty-two."

"They're not considered as friends in this. Aaron is your horse. A gorgeous black stallion, running, muscles rippling, but he does what he wants at times. As you said."

"I'll say wow again. You're really onto something. This is impressive."

For the first time since the idea came to her, she realized that this might have been a good move. Vivian had agreed with it, but in Sarah's heart, she still wasn't sure. The therapist is another human being, one with struggles and a troubled childhood, most likely. Therapists spend their day buying groceries, dealing with irate drivers on the road, and day-to-day stressors just like the rest of the human race. With everyone just trying to get through each day and enter the next alive and healthy, getting psychological help after what she had been through in her short life didn't feel right somehow. But Vivian's thoughts haunted her, and Vivian could do nothing about it. So the idea of talking to someone had come up, and Sarah reluctantly agreed. Hence the idea of a two-month escape.

"The flowers are the only ones that disturbed me," Williams said.

"How's that?"

"Have you ever been pregnant before?"

Sarah shook her head. "No. Absolutely not."

Williams rubbed his chin as he looked down at the pad. "Flowers represent how you feel about children."

"I love children," she snapped. "I always put children first."

"Not children in general." He looked at her. "Your children. You saw the lilies by a grave. That tells me the idea of having children for you is dead. You're so convinced you'll never have children that you've buried the idea, figuratively speaking."

Sarah shook her head in the negative. "Not so. I plan on kids one day, just not yet. When you asked about flowers, I said lilies because those were the flowers I left at my sister's grave yesterday. You would've gotten a different answer if you had asked these questions a week ago."

"Okay. Then let's move on. The storm represents problems in your life. Since this storm is directly over your head, sometimes raining, sometimes not, that tells me your problems are always there, preying on you."

"Tell me about it."

"There's lightning, dark clouds, and blackness."

"The lightning must be gunfire," Sarah said, trying to gauge his reaction. If she continued with this doctor, he would learn of her lifestyle fast enough. Gauging his reaction would help her decide how much to reveal going forward.

He continued talking as if he didn't hear her comment. "But here's something interesting. You said it was the storm and the rain that ruined the ladder years ago." He looked up at her. "That means you've allowed your problems to push your friends away."

"That makes sense, but it didn't happen exactly like that."

He set his pad aside. "The point of that exercise is to allow me to see where you're at. To see how your relationships are coming along. How you are with friends, with Aaron, and what is bothering you in life. Of course, it's all general, surface detail, but without asking you directly, I can get to know you better. It enables me to have a firm grasp on where you're at, which only allows me to guide you through whatever it is you have come to talk about."

"Okay, now that we have that out of the way, I prefer a more direct approach in the future. Ask me anything, and I'll answer or choose not to."

"I assure you, the beauty of these questions isn't to trip you up. It's to assess you psychologically without the awkwardness of me asking how you and your friends are getting along. Or what you think of Aaron. Now I have a solid opinion of how you feel about Aaron."

"Okay, I admit, I like how it played out, but I'm more of a straight shooter. Let's just play our cards and see how the game unfolds. It's my dime, after all."

"Agreed." He adjusted his seat, switched his position to face her better, and picked up his pen. "Do you have any questions for me? Or would you like to discuss why you're here?"

A door shut hard on the floor below them. Because Dr. Williams's office was the only one on this floor, the sound echoed throughout the mostly hollow building. Outside, the sun had moved enough for her to see that the Ford was as dark as the one from yesterday.

Is it the same? she asked Vivian.

"There's a lot to be said about the chair you choose in my office," Williams added.

Sarah turned back to him. "Oh yeah? What's this chair say about me?"

Her stomach twitched, and her palms moistened with sweat. She hadn't been in action since the murder of Father

Adams in a hospital in Los Angeles almost nine months ago. She forgot how it felt.

It was evident that someone was following her. But who? And why?

And why was Vivian silent on the matter?

Unless this was Vivian's plan all along.

Are you leading me to Cole Lincoln? she asked Vivian.

Another door banged below them.

Something changed on the doctor's face. Was it fear? Or anger?

Sarah was sure she'd find out soon enough.

Her phone vibrated in her pants again.

Chapter 6

After Sarah failed to pick up his call again, Aaron checked his speed and slowed down. Getting pulled over and attracting police attention would only piss Sarah off more than she already would be when she saw him.

Sure, he had to get used to her ways, how she didn't want him looking over her shoulder, watching her back. She looked at it like he was interfering. But for their relationship to work, she also had to get used to his ways. When he receives a message like the one she left on his cell, she can't possibly expect him to continue to drive the other way. Of course, he would come back.

People watching the cabin. Male footprints in the dirt outside the cabin's window.

He smacked the dash.

"No way am I leaving her alone."

His cell rang. He hit the button on the dash that routed it

through the car's stereo speakers.

"Yeah?" he said.

"You there yet?" Parkman asked.

"Ten more minutes."

"Okay. I tied up everything I was working on here. I'll come out and meet you at the cabin. I'll need a few hours."

"Just keep in touch. I'll tell you where I am when you're in the area."

"Okay. Text me when you have Sarah."

"There could be a delay."

"Why?"

"Sarah had her first doctor's appointment this morning. She may not be back from that for a few hours if she decides to run errands after or something."

"Fine. Just update me when you have something. I'm on my way."

"Hey, Parkman? What were you working on?"

"You really want to know?"

"Yeah."

"A woman hired me to follow her husband."

"Why?"

"Suspicion of adultery."

"Was he?"

"Yeah."

"Thought so."

"Cynical much?"

"No. Real."

"Whatever. I'm on my way."

"Hurry."

Aaron disconnected the call. He checked his mirrors, saw no one behind him, then added pressure to the pedal.

Chapter 7

"Do you know the car in the parking lot over there?" Sarah asked. She got up from the chair and pointed out the window.

Dr. Williams remained seated. He tapped his pen a few times against his knee.

"What is there to fear, Sarah? It's daytime. The sun is high. We're in an office complex off the beaten path where it's quiet and relaxing. A calm place to talk. To heal. What is it you came to discuss with me?"

"How long have you been here?" Sarah asked.

"I understood your visit today was about you, not me."

"Where was your office located before moving into this one?" The wall behind his desk had framed diplomas hung high, but she hadn't examined a single one of them upon entering.

"Are you looking for legitimacy? Am I who I say I am?"

"That would be a start." The nervous twitch in her

stomach had subsided. Not so much because she was less nervous, but because she was taking action, doing what she knew best.

"I would be happy to supply you with my academic history and credits as a psychologist, but first, I'm curious. How did you find me? Why book an appointment, chat with me for almost half an hour, and then suddenly question my integrity? What have I done that changed your mind?"

"It's what you're not doing."

"And what is that, Sarah?"

She fixed him with a stare, eyeing him up and down until she was convinced he wasn't there to help her. Maybe she had been out of this game for too long. Had rust formed on her instincts?

"You're not answering my question about that car out there."

"Are you afraid of the car or its owner?"

"Not much scares me, really." She hesitated a moment, then continued. "Yesterday, Aaron and I drove out to my sister's grave. A car like that one," she pointed again, "was in the cemetery."

"I'm sure they, too, had lost a loved one."

"We saw them again when we left. Then someone was snooping around my residence last night."

"I'm not sure I can help you," Williams said. He set the pad aside and got up from his chair. "This kind of matter is one for the police."

Something about his demeanor offended her. How could he deduce such a thing in such a small amount of time? "Why's that?" she asked.

He walked around his desk. "Because the load of guilt

you must carry on your shoulders, the years of toil and trouble, as Shakespeare would say, amount to something I'm not interested in discussing. As clients get to interview their doctors, so do doctors get the same privilege."

She frowned, then smiled. "So we're done here?"

"Not exactly."

She moved to the other side of his desk and faced him, trying to figure out what was happening. Earlier, he had acted strange. Now his demeanor was more aggressive like he knew her and was upset about something. She didn't understand it, nor could she put a finger on it.

Vivian? You there? Watching this?

"How are we not done yet? You just dismissed me as a client."

"No, I didn't. I said I'm not sure I can help you."

"My point exactly." She crossed her arms.

"But a team of doctors could."

That surprised her. "What?"

A presence materialized behind her. She spun around, ducked low, and prepared to strike. There were two burly men with Russian-like faces who flanked her. Each one stepped back, their hands raised.

Her right thigh stung with the quick movement.

She pointed at the men; sure, they were the same two from yesterday.

"Step back more. Both of you. We need to discuss a few things." She turned back to Dr. Williams while keeping her eyes on the newcomers. "These two work for you?"

"Not exactly."

"You were spying on me?"

"No, I wasn't."

"What's going on here?" She moved to the side where she could watch the doctor and the two men, who were now a safe distance away.

"Who are you two? Why did you follow me yesterday? Were you at my cabin last night?"

She felt light-headed. The room spun for a moment. When she looked back at the doctor, he was leaning back in his large leather office chair, a smug look on his face.

"I fucking well want answers! What is this? Who are you? Do I know you?"

She faltered, catching the desk's edge before falling to the floor. Her thigh stung again.

Looking down at it, she saw the needle still embedded, all the way in, plunger depressed.

How did they ...?

A raging fury surged through her as she tried to block whatever was in the needle from working on her.

"You'll pay for this," she said to the doctor.

Then she turned to the pair of large men as she yanked the needle out of her leg. Holding it above her, she advanced on them.

They dared to smile as if the little girl with the empty needle could really do any harm.

Bones break on men so easily. Soon, no more smiling ...

She didn't make it halfway across the office floor before she collapsed.

Through the muddled fog in her head, she heard them talking, discussing plans.

"Go now," the doctor said. "Trash the cabin. Find anything you can that'll link back to us and destroy it. I'll take care of the stupid girl. Go!"

As hard as she tried to push up off the floor, it felt like she weighed a thousand pounds. Nothing would respond or move.

Not even her eyelids once they'd closed.

Being awake even seemed too heavy to contemplate.

And Sarah was out.

Chapter 8

AARON SKIDDED TO A halt in front of the cabin. There was no sign of Sarah's car.

Of course, not.

She would still be at her doctor's appointment. He didn't have a key to the cabin and didn't want to wait in the car until she returned. He got out and did a perimeter check of the area. He saw the footprints Sarah talked about in her message. He also saw animal paw prints.

Back at the front of the cabin, with the distant sound of traffic on the highway a mile away, Aaron tried the front door.

Locked.

Then he walked around the cabin again, this time trying each window. They were all upgraded in recent years. Nothing budged. Short of taking a crowbar and breaking a window or picking a lock, there was no way he was getting inside the cabin.

He walked back to his car and leaned his forearms on the roof.

What now?

He grabbed his cell phone and tried Sarah's number again.

No answer.

He called Parkman.

"Parkman here."

"I'm at the cabin."

"And?"

"Sarah's not here. I see the prints she referred to in her message, but nobody's here, and the place is locked up solid. I couldn't tell from outside, but as far as I know, this place has an alarm. Sarah would've set it when she left."

"And no one else is around? You didn't see any indication of someone watching the place?"

"I didn't look for that."

"Aaron. If someone is hunting Sarah—I mean, she has created a lot of friends over the past seven years, but a lot of enemies, too—you could be a sitting duck right now."

"I'm fine. No one's here."

The sound of wind came through the phone. Parkman was in his car, on his way.

"Today was Sarah's doctor's meeting, right?" Parkman asked.

"Yes."

"Where?"

"No idea. She kept that to herself."

"I don't like this."

"Me neither."

"Get inside."

"What?"

"Get inside the cabin."

"How?"

"Figure it out. Just get inside. Look around. Find the doctor's address. As soon as you have it, text it to me. I'll have someone look into this guy."

Aaron was on the move.

"Also, Aaron."

"Yeah?"

"See if there's anything else you can discover. Is she working on something? Has Vivian tasked her to do something important? Maybe get into her computer. Do you know her passwords?"

"Some of them. Not all. But she's going to be pissed." He stopped at the front door and gripped the handle.

"Yes, she will be pissed, but we'll survive this. If she's in trouble, then she needs us. If there's no trouble, we'll treat her to dinner and drill into her head that we love her. One day she'll get it."

Aaron almost laughed. "Yeah, one day. Which day? Could you predict one in particular?"

Parkman ignored his sarcasm. "I'm just over an hour away. Text me when you have something."

"Done."

Aaron hung up, slipped the phone into his back pocket, and stepped closer to examine the door, looking for its weak spot.

Directly above the handle looked like the best place.

He turned until his left side faced the door. Then, in a quick snap, he lifted his right leg, folded at the waist, and spun his right foot back and around to connect with the door at the exact spot above the knob. The wood cracked, and a vertical line formed in the wood.

He brought his foot back, lifted it high, and swung it again, connecting with the same spot.

The door popped, wood moaning in protest. He looked inside, then crossed the threshold. The alarm sounded, a shrill cry from a loudspeaker somewhere inside and outside.

He scanned the alarm panel beside the door, but it was new. None of the buttons showed wear.

"Dammit."

He ran for the back of the cabin, looking for a utility room of some sort. Finally, the ear-splitting sharp noise from the alarm ceased. His ears rang in the aftermath.

The alarm panel on the wall by the front door continued to beep from the violation.

In the bathroom, he found the alarm box and the speaker.

It was locked.

He punched it twice until the small metal door buckled enough to pop it open. As he did this, the piercing alarm sounded again, but now the speaker was one foot from his head.

He tore at the wires and their connections and continued to do this until the last one killed the speaker's horrendous noise. He sat back to collect himself. Then the phone rang.

It had to be the monitoring station calling to get a code or something. When they didn't get someone on the phone, police would be dispatched.

"Shit, this was a stupid idea. Thanks, Parkman. I owe you one for this."

He ripped the phone cord out of the wall.

The ringing in the main part of the cabin died.

"Sarah's going to be more than pissed."

He stepped out of the bathroom and took in the cabin. Everything looked as normal as it could be. Her Stephen King novel, *Mr. Mercedes*, was on the coffee table. Her MacBook Pro was on the kitchen table. An empty bottle of wine sat on the counter beside one used wine glass.

Inside the bedroom, the bed was made with no clothes scattered about. Other than the wine glass, the cabin was spotless, just as he would've expected from Sarah.

He sat at the kitchen table and opened her laptop computer's screen. It lit, and the password icon popped up.

He tried Sarah's name with no success. Then he tried his own. Then combinations of their names. He tried her birthdate, her parents' names, and Vivian's birthdate, but nothing succeeded.

Tapping his fingers on the table, he tried to imagine what she would use as a password.

Then it occurred to him.

Vivian's name.

Short and simple. It meant something to Sarah, but hardly anyone else would ever know that name except family and her few friends.

Vivian's name worked.

Her desktop popped up.

Something made a rustling sound in the room behind him. He stopped what he was doing and looked over his shoulder. He knew he was alone in the cabin. As long as he had been here, no one had pulled up the driveway. He would've heard them. Unless they pulled in when the alarm was blaring, how would anyone get past him and into the bedroom?

It was nothing, he thought, dismissing the sound.

The front door hung wide open. He could see out to his car. He was alone.

His attention drawn back to her computer, he brought up her browser and searched through its history. Research on Cole Lincoln, page after page.

Then he brought up her email program. She had four new emails.

One from Apple announcing a new, thinner MacBook Air. Two from writing websites as she had taken to writing her memoirs more seriously lately. And the fourth was from a woman named Rebecca Lincoln.

"Rebecca Lincoln," Aaron said out loud.

Related to Cole?

He opened the email and scanned the long letter. The beginning spoke of things going wrong for her brother.

Cole's her brother?

He lost his job. Suspected of crimes committed while on duty. A police officer was murdered. No one knows who did it. The case remains unsolved. Other horrible things happened. Underage girls were molested after an illegal brothel was raided.

Holy shit!

Her brother ended up in—

There was the distinctive sound of a footstep behind him.

Impossible.

He moved his eyes, nothing else. The outside, through the broken-in door, was still clear. Only his car sat out front.

A rustle of clothes.

Definitely, someone was behind him.

Sarah? It couldn't be.

She wouldn't sneak up on him like that. Too risky for both of them.

He kicked his chair backward violently and dropped to the floor sideways. Landing on his shoulder, he spun around to see who had snuck up on him.

A tall, well-built man in a leather jacket stood over him, a syringe in his hands.

"Well, now, who the fuck are you?" Aaron asked.

But he didn't wait for an answer. Trained in the art of Shotokan Karate, a black belt who had trained others for years as a teacher in his own dojo in Toronto, Aaron stayed calm when sparring. Even though the man startled him, Aaron took advantage instantly. He kicked the chair toward the man before he could move. Using the forward motion of his legs, he drove his other heel hard at the man's shin.

The contact was solid. The man buckled as his lower leg thrust backward. Aaron was already spinning away. He pushed up and off the floor, landing on his feet in a crouched position.

More footsteps in the cabin. Someone else was here.

How many?

He prepared for the fight, tightened his fists, released them, and stepped forward, his eyes roaming the living room and kitchen of the cabin.

The second man ran out of the bedroom. Aaron dodged left. He was right-handed, as were the majority of his sparring partners. Most dodge to the right, so moving left would be unexpected.

It worked. The second man, also in a black leather jacket, expected him to go to the right. As soon as he ran past, missing Aaron in his open-armed tackle attempt, Aaron focused on the first man with the needle.

He had lifted the chair over his head, and the man threw the chair before Aaron could maneuver out of the way.

He covered his head, arms up, locked together to support themselves upon contact, and squeezed his eyes shut.

The chair's front legs smacked Aaron's forearms. He hoped the crack was wood and not bone.

He opened his eyes, spun away from the chair as it fell, and dropped low into his shuto, hands at the ready, equilibrium centered.

Man number two had spun around after running past Aaron and was already headed his way.

Two large men in close quarters could be trouble. He needed to drop one fast.

It took two seconds for man number two to be within reach. Aaron snapped out his right hand and connected with the man's throat hard enough to cause breathing issues but no collapse of the trachea.

The man crumpled forward into Aaron. He no longer reached for Aaron as his hands now clung to the front of his neck, but his weight drove Aaron back into the wall.

Man number one was on the move. He jumped over the downed chair, raised the hand with the needle, and brought it down toward Aaron's stomach.

With his feet still tangled under the weight of man number two, all Aaron could do was fend off the needle from his awkward position against the wall. Quick as he could, he smacked the man's hand away, hoping to dislodge the offending syringe. As it sailed away, his gaze following it to confirm it was out of action, he failed to see man number one's fist come from the other side.

His vision faltered at the impact, stars coalesced in place of the cabin, and his balance shifted.

Then another fist came from the other side. His head got hit twice as it bounced off the wall beside him.

He fought to keep on his feet. He thrust his arms out in a defensive attack, but somehow another fist, or what felt like a chunk of stone, walloped him behind the ear, and the stars were replaced by darkness as he slumped down the wall and crumpled to the floor.

The last conscious thought was one word.

Sarah ...

Chapter 9

"AARON?" A FAMILIAR VOICE. "Come on, open your eyes. It's Parkman."

Aaron shot his hands up, eyes blinking rapidly to clear the fuzziness. He was outside. Lying down. The sun was still up, the air warm.

Parkman had stepped back, remaining a safe distance. Police cars were on the property. An ambulance with its lights flashing sat ten yards away.

"You feeling okay?" Parkman asked.

"Sarah?" Aaron said.

Parkman shook his head. A policeman with a thick midsection and mustache to match stepped up beside Parkman.

"We were hoping you would know something," the officer said. "Like, who did this?" He gestured at the cabin.

Aaron coughed, cleared his throat, and sat up. A

paramedic moved close, but Aaron waved him off.

"Got any water?"

Parkman nodded and slipped inside the cabin. He returned a moment later and handed a glass of water to Aaron. After a long drink, he got to his feet. The side of his head ached, but that was all he felt. He was lucky they didn't do worse.

"Two guys," Aaron started. The cop took out a notepad and started to write. "Two big guys. Black leather jackets. Don't know how they got in. Waiting for me—"

"It's obvious how they got in," Parkman interjected. "They busted through the front door and ripped all the alarm wires out of the panel in the bathroom."

A plainclothes officer walked up. "I'm Nick Kershaw. And no, I don't sing."

"Huh?"

He shook his head to brush off the comment. "Parkman is an old colleague. Most of us know him from years ago." Kershaw snuck an admiring glance at Parkman. "And read about his time in Los Angeles last year." He looked back at Aaron. "He said he was talking to you on your cell as you approached the building." The other officer with the thick mustache held his pen poised over the pad, waiting for Aaron to speak.

Parkman offered an almost imperceptible nod.

"Two guys came out of nowhere. Surprised me. I tried to fight back."

"It's okay," Parkman said as he put an arm around Aaron's shoulder. "At least they left you alone once you were knocked out."

Aaron glanced inside the cabin. It had been ransacked,

completely destroyed. The couch was torn apart and flipped upside down. The table was broken into multiple pieces, and the counters were slashed. Papers, garbage, and Sarah's computer parts scattered the floor. The only thing left intact was the Stephen King book Sarah had been reading. It sat like an island of sanity amongst the ruins of a destructive force.

"Did you hear anything?" Kershaw asked. "See anything that would help us locate Miss Sarah Roberts?"

Aaron turned back and looked into his eyes. "I wish I did. That's why I came here. Sarah called me last night."

"What call?"

Parkman gave him a stern look, but Aaron didn't have the same level of distrust of the cops as Sarah and Parkman seemed to share. Sure, some of them were assholes, but having more information might help.

"She left me a message this morning about the footprints she'd discovered surrounding the cabin. She thought she heard something last night. When she went out to investigate, a deer was in the yard. It wasn't until this morning that she found evidence of someone else's presence."

"Do you know where she was supposed to be today?"

"A doctor's appointment," Parkman piped in. "She should be back soon."

"After this," Kershaw pointed at the cabin again, "and someone watching her last night, who knows where she is or when she'll be back. I'll get this in, and, hey Aaron, do you have a current photo of Sarah?"

"Not on me."

"Okay, I'll contact her parents for an up-to-date photo. We'll get it out to every unit in the state if she shows up, great. If not, we'll do everything we can to find her."

"Thanks," Parkman said and shook Kershaw's hand.

They stepped away, and Parkman led Aaron for a walk around the building. At the back, he said, "Tell me what happened. We have to find Sarah before they do."

"Why?" Aaron looked at him. "What do you know that I don't?"

"You know how Sarah feels about cops in general."

"I thought her hatred of them was over. Look at what she just did in Los Angeles."

"Hatred lasts a long time. The whole reason she's in this cabin and seeing that shrink—"

"Not shrink," Aaron said.

"Okay, psychiatrist, although Sarah and I have different opinions of them, it's because of what a cop did to her. Now, this happens, and cops come looking for her. It's just the one time she wants to take two months to herself, read, relax, sleep in, do whatever she needs to do to be able to quiet her mind with Vivian in there rummaging around, and then this happens. Not good."

"On that, I agree."

"Thanks for thinking fast back there. Now that the story is the guys who attacked you broke in, you're no longer in a wringer."

They walked to the perimeter of the lot. Aaron leaned against a tree, still trying to clear his head.

"What can you tell me?" Parkman asked.

"After silencing the alarm, I fired up her laptop. I found nothing of interest until I discovered an email from Rebecca Lincoln."

"Lincoln? As in Cole Lincoln?"

Aaron nodded. "The sister."

"Really? Sounds like Sarah was onto something."

"Rebecca was responding to Sarah's email. Said something about Cole getting into trouble. Someone was murdered. He lost his job. Underage prostitutes and corruption charges or something like that. Rebecca had written where Cole is, but then I detected someone behind me." He shook his head in dismay.

"What?"

"I just don't know how they got the jump on me. No one was here when I broke in. The alarm was on. They couldn't already be inside."

Two officers walked around the back of the cabin and stopped to examine the rear window. Once they moved off, Parkman turned to face him again.

"The alarm panel is in the bathroom. How long were you in there trying to disable the siren?"

"A whole minute, maybe more."

"Couldn't they have run in during that minute and then hid in the bedroom until you were seated at the table, refocused on the computer?"

"I guess so. But I should've beat them, though. I'm faster, lighter, and can think better on my feet."

"Even black belts take a beating sometimes."

"They had a needle. Tried to stick me with it."

Parkman tilted his head back and raised his eyebrows. "Really? That adds a twist to things."

"Maybe these cops"—Aaron waved his arm—"will find it in the mess in there and can analyze it."

"Hope so. Would love to know what they were carrying. It could help locate the source and, in turn, lead us to them because, at this point, we have no idea who we're after or where Sarah is."

A soft breeze picked up, cooling Aaron. "Did Sarah give you the doctor's name or location? Anything?"

"She said something about it being above a lawyer's office. Maybe a half-hour drive from here. The doctor's safe, though. Vivian recommended him."

"Vivian?"

"Yeah."

Officer Kershaw came running around the building, his face red and stressed. "There you are," he shouted. "We have to leave. You guys want a ride along?"

"Where are we going?" Parkman asked.

"A woman's body was just found inside a Dodge Charger in the parking lot of a lawyer's office. After the call came in, my guy checked the plates and called me. This particular Dodge Charger is registered to Sarah Roberts. I'm sorry. Thought you guys might want to see what's going on firsthand. And if it's Sarah, I'll need a positive ID."

The pit of Aaron's stomach dropped and twirled and spun in circles. Aaron started humming as he stepped behind Parkman, as they followed the cop to his car.

"Why are you humming?" Parkman asked.

"Because it's pretty hard to gag while humming."

Parkman looked back over his shoulder. "You're going to gag?"

"No. Throw up. Trying not to."

"Please don't. It's not Sarah in that car. Everything will work out. Just chill."

Aaron hummed until the cabin was out of sight.

Chapter 10

KERSHAW'S POLICE CAR SCREECHED to a halt in the parking lot, twenty feet behind Sarah's Dodge. They couldn't go any farther as state trooper cruisers and other emergency personnel littered the lot.

The coroner was already on site. Kershaw, with Aaron and Parkman following close, exited the cruiser and moved toward Sarah's car.

White-coated men were inside the Charger. Aaron's heart sank as he recognized it as Sarah's. The entire fifteen minutes it took to get there, he hoped and prayed it wouldn't be Sarah's car and that there had been some kind of mix-up. But his prayers went unanswered.

The woman being worked on had dark brown hair, almost black. Aaron and Parkman had arrived in time to watch as they extricated the body from the front seat of Sarah's car. The heavyset woman was definitely not Sarah.

Then he remembered something.

"Parkman, you said Sarah was meeting a doctor above a lawyer's office. Sarah's car is here." Aaron pointed to the second floor of the brown office building. "And you said it was about a half-hour drive from the cabin." He stepped in front of Parkman. "This is it. Sarah pulled in here this morning. Maybe the doctor's around. He could know something."

Parkman walked past him, accidentally bumping his shoulder as he went. Aaron watched him approach the officer in charge. Parkman got animated as he explained that they needed to enter the building.

Aaron moved closer to hear better.

"But it's sealed off," the officer said. "Only our guys are getting inside. This is a crime scene."

"You have to make an exception. We need to get upstairs, talk to the doctor, or at least get contact information."

The cop shook his head. "Not going to happen. Although I have no idea as to what you're referring to. There are no offices on the second floor. It's all under renovation."

Aaron stared up at the windows on the second floor, paying attention to what he could see on the inside. Unfinished walls, plastic wrapped in front of insulation, stickers still on the new panes of the windows. On the main floor, the door that led to the upstairs displayed a building permit.

"Is there even an office on the second floor?" Aaron asked loud enough for the officer in charge to hear.

"It's being renovated. There's only a lawyer's office on the ground floor. That's it."

Parkman trudged back to Aaron. "What now?" he asked.

"No idea. Sarah's gone. There's a body in her car, and we have no idea where to look for her."

"Let's work out what we do know."

Officer Kershaw moved into their inner circle. "I'll help if I can," he said. "Let's hear what you have so far."

Aaron met Parkman's eyes. He blinked back once, slowly.

It's okay. This guy's cool.

Aaron nodded. "Sarah was supposed to meet a doctor today. The second floor of a lawyer's office. A half-hour drive from the cabin." He pointed at the Charger. "Her car's here." He updated them once more on what happened when he got jumped until they arrived here. "But there's something else. Yesterday, Sarah and I drove out to visit her sister's gravesite."

"And?" Kershaw prompted.

"Two men in dark leather jackets, like those who jumped me today, were visiting another grave. After we left the cemetery, they passed us in their car. Sarah was sure they were watching us. She asked me if I thought so, too. I didn't think they were and now realize I should've listened to her."

"What were they driving?" Kershaw asked.

"A black Ford Fusion."

"Anything else?"

Aaron shook his head.

"I'll call it in and have my guys watching for two men in a Fusion. It's not much, but it's better than nothing."

He strode back to his cruiser and hopped in the front seat.

"We'll find her, Aaron," Parkman said.

"I hope so, but we've got nothing. I just hope she can handle whatever she's going through on her own."

"Me too, Aaron. Me too."

Chapter 11

SOMETHING DUG INTO HER ankles and wrists. At first, it was a bother, but now that her head was clearing, the ache intensified. A headache the size of Everest was booming from temple to temple in an attempt to open her skull in whichever spot she might desire.

Bedsheets ruffled under her slightest movements. She became alert to her body and mentally examined it for injuries. Her thigh was a little sore from the way the needle was violently slammed in but other than that, her headache was the only pain trying to rip her apart from the inside.

She opened her eyes and immediately jammed them shut. Cranial pressure seemed to double in that single motion. The lights above her bed shone inside her head and elevated the pain to white hot.

What the hell?

"I see you're waking up."

She didn't open her eyes. Just turned her head toward the sound. The voice belonged to the fake doctor who trapped her. Dr. Lance Williams.

"How long have I been here?" she whispered.

"You're not interested in knowing where here is first?" the doctor asked.

"I already know where I am."

"Where's that?"

"The building you die in. I'm good with that. How long I've been here is another thing entirely." Talking worsened her migraine, but some things were more important than pain.

"Pray tell. Why does the length of your stay matter?"

"It'll tell me how much backup I'll have coming through that door when I'm ready to leave."

"I can honestly say I've never met anyone with your tenacity. You lie on a bed, and your wrists and ankles are secured with strong leather straps. You're drugged. No one knows where you are, and you can't leave, yet you're talking as if I'm the prisoner. Wow, you've got some nerve, kid."

She smiled, then tried to open her eyes. The pain flared and forced her eyes shut. She yanked up on her wrists and pulled her knees back, but all four restraints held tight.

"You can't get out," Williams said. "There is no escape from here."

"Why am I *here*?" she asked. Then, under her breath, "Wherever here is."

"You are here because, as a doctor, I have the power to commit you involuntarily for a seventy-two-hour hold according to California's Mental Health laws. After you threatened suicide—"

"I did no such thing."

"Funny," he said, his voice moving as he walked toward the end of the bed. "After you injected yourself with a foreign substance in my office, I had no other option but to bring you in for observation. You were acting deranged. Said something about killing a woman. You presented a case to me, a designated mental health professional, that you were a danger to yourself and possibly a danger to others."

"You know as well as I do that your men injected me, and I never once spoke of killing anyone. What is this all about? Revenge? Betrayal? Money? Come on, you can tell me, what have I done to offend thee?"

"It's not me you've offended, as you so elegantly put it. But I'm sure you'll meet him soon enough. Lastly, your denial will go on record. Your refusal to see the need for help. After your seventy-two-hour stay, unless you show signs of regaining your mental health, I can invoke a fourteen-day hold. Who knows? Maybe you'll be classified as gravely disabled, and I'll order a thirty-day hold after that. Wouldn't it be nice? Spend almost the next two months locked up on this bed, injected routinely in different areas of your pretty little body if you know what I mean."

His threats drew concern, but focusing on them would anger her and ultimately give him the power to keep her, as she would become a danger to others, namely him.

Her eyes remained closed. She let her mind wander, trying hard to come up with a name. The name of the person who could orchestrate this or had the power to. Most of the people she had dealt with that would want her dead were already dead. Maybe it was a relative of a long-ago enemy.

"You're in the Amy Greg Psychiatric Hospital," Williams

said. "The office of patients' rights is in Sacramento, about three hours' drive from here. I've looked you up online. Since you're such a badass, a danger to others"—he used air quotes on *danger*—"I won't let you get your required phone call. Although I am legally bound to tell you, this is not a criminal arrest." He slapped his hands together as if to brush crumbs off them. "There, I've done what was required of me to keep you."

As if to back up that claim that she was in a psychiatric ward, someone shouted a warbled cry from beyond the walls of her room until it was suddenly cut off.

"You're in the acute ward for the mentally ill," he said.

Sarah rolled her head toward his voice. She opened her eyes to slits without too much pain flaring. "Which means?"

"The acute ward is for people who are very ill. Some refer to it as the 'long-stay' ward. You're in the sectioned-off area, or what we call legally detained. Some call it the back ward, or *backward*." He touched her leg below the knee. She fought the urge to pull away, not that she could. Sympathy had no time for weakness in a place like this. Only strength survived in this world.

His hand began to move upward, slowly. "Even if you managed to get out of those restraints, this room will be locked, and the doors at each end of the corridor will be secured. The entire area is locked down. Before your seventy-two-hour involuntary committal is through, I will file the appropriate documents that explain my findings and how I deem you chronically ill." His hand rested on the top of her right thigh now. It began to move again. "You will never leave this building." His hand stopped beside her vagina, just below her protruding hip bone. Every fiber in her body ached to drive a fist down his throat and into his stomach.

His hand brushed softly between her legs before he removed it. Then it landed on her right breast, his lips close to her ear. "You will never leave this building," he repeated. "But before you kill yourself, as is the plan, the man responsible for your stay with us wants to enjoy your lady parts. I understand he's had his way with you before, so he's quite familiar with the terrain. Although you're older now. He may not like that, but it won't matter much to you."

He moved away from her ear. His hand left her breast. "You'll spend the last week of your life drugged and fucked. Doesn't that sound wonderful? And in the end, I'll come out of this a hero as I committed you here in the wasted effort of trying to save your life."

Sarah remained silent, her anger making her pant now. The headache subsided some in the wake of her fury.

A door opened.

"You can come in now."

Two pairs of footsteps entered the room. She opened her eyes enough to see two men dressed in white lab coats, one with a needle, the other carrying more leather straps.

"These men," the doctor continued, "will help with the pain. Soon you'll sleep. But first, these men must take your clothes and burn them." He turned to the orderlies. "Inject her first." He turned to stare into Sarah's slitted eyes. "She's feisty. A severe danger to herself and others. Once she's out, rip her clothes off, secure her to the bed as tight as possible without cutting off circulation, and leave her hospital clothes in the corner. I'll help her dress when she's awake tomorrow."

They nodded in unison. "Yes, sir. But leave her naked?"

"That's what I said. She's too much of a suicide risk. Somehow she'll find a way to take her gown off and have it around her neck within minutes if I don't dress her myself. Leave her naked for the world to see." He winked at Sarah. "I'll be back soon." He opened the door to leave. "I'm suddenly looking forward to seeing you again."

The door was about to close. One of the orderlies lifted a syringe and pushed the plunger a notch. Clear liquid spit out the tip.

"Doctor?" Sarah said as the door finally closed. Williams stuck his head back in.

"What is it?"

"You will die in this room. Come back here at your own peril."

For a brief moment, his eyes flickered. She saw caution, possibly fear.

He smiled. "I highly doubt that." The door closed.

It all came to Sarah in a rush. She was looking for Cole Lincoln, her old babysitter who had abused her all those years ago. Her search had proven to be a daunting task as she couldn't find him. And now she was here, waiting to meet the person who, as Williams said, *has had his way with you before*. That could only mean Lincoln was here and had orchestrated this entire thing.

The needle entered her right arm. She jerked in surprise.

The ankle restraints came off, but she suddenly had no fight left in her. Whatever was in the needle worked incredibly fast.

Now she understood why Vivian said it would all work out in its own time. That was why she recommended Dr. Williams, who was, in fact, a real doctor, as Sarah had discovered through her background checks. But how would Cole know she would go to Williams and that Williams could be bought? How Cole fit in was a mystery and one she intended to figure out before it was too late.

The pain in her head decreased to almost nothing as a wave of sleep rolled over her.

After what happened to her before she was a teenager and what happened to her sister, she had enough resolve to go after Cole with a fierce vengeance. Lately, with Vivian's memories haunting her, Cole was all Sarah thought about.

The threat of another event to mirror the past, another rape, would be too much. She would be haunted for as long as she lived if that happened to her as she lay helpless, strapped to a bed.

She had all the mental ammunition she needed to go after men like Cole. She didn't need another *event* to give her more ammunition.

All another *event* would do to her …

She lost the thought as her shirt was torn from her body. At some point, her wrists were released from the straps. She was completely free of the bed and had no strength to do anything about it.

Her bra was removed. Something cold pressed against her side by her buttock. Scissors. Then her panties were removed easily.

Oh, Vivian … where are you …

Whatever they injected in her arm took complete hold. For once in her life, it was a pleasure to go under. When she surfaced, she would deal with whatever came her way then.

And what was that he said about a dead woman?

But for now, naked in a mental ward, demented

caregivers planning their next move, being forced to nod off kept her from ridiculing her sister for not giving her any notice or warning.

What the fuck is this, sis?

Chapter 12

"WE HAVE TO GET a MacBook Pro," Aaron said. "And we have to do it immediately."

They stood in the shade at the back of the parking lot as the Dodge Charger was dusted for prints. The lawyer's office was closed, and Kershaw was waiting for the key holder to arrive and allow them a tour of the premises.

"Why?" Parkman asked.

"Because we have no other leads." Aaron wiped the sweat from his brow and rubbed it on his jeans. "Wherever Sarah is, she needs us. As far as we know, Sarah could be five minutes from here or already crossing state lines. The last clue to where she is will be on her computer."

"But her computer's completely smashed—" Parkman's eyes widened. "That's why you want another MacBook. So you can back up her hard drive from that Time Capsule thing she uses."

"Exactly."

"Okay, let's go. They don't need us here."

Parkman left Aaron alone so he could call a taxi while he strode over to tell Kershaw they were leaving.

Moments later, he returned. "Kershaw has my cell number, and I've got his," Parkman said.

"Great. Cab'll meet us two blocks from here."

"Why two blocks?"

Aaron shrugged. "Don't know. Just didn't want to be picked up at a murder scene."

Parkman frowned. "Hmmph. Okay."

They left the shade and started walking. It was hot for late April, warning them that the coming summer could be a scorcher. The yellow taxi came up the street. Aaron waved, and the vehicle veered toward them, stopping two feet away.

Parkman grabbed the door handle but didn't open it. "How much of that email from Cole's sister did you get to read?"

"Over half of it. Rebecca was about to tell Sarah where Cole is. I'm assuming Sarah read the email last night. Once we read the email, we might know where Sarah has gone."

Aaron got in the taxi. Parkman followed.

"Take us to town. We need an Apple Store."

The unshaven driver, whose cab reeked of cigarette smoke, twisted in his seat and looked at Aaron. "You mean apples and oranges, as in fruit? Or Apples, as in computers?"

"Computers."

"This might prove difficult," the driver said.

"How so?" Parkman asked.

"Not many people around here can afford an Apple. The closest store is in the big city. Many hours from here. We could drive south and reach Sacramento in three to four hours."

Aaron shot a side glance at Parkman. "Now what?"

"It has to be a Mac?" Parkman asked.

Aaron nodded. "We can't sit on the highway in a taxi for almost eight hours there and back to the cabin, buy a thousand-dollar computer, and transfer the files over an eight-hour period so we can read one email. That's too long. Sarah doesn't have that long."

"Is there an internet café anywhere?" Parkman asked.

The driver shook his head in the negative, the taxi still idling. Then said, "There is, but it has old PCs, not Macs."

"We need to take it to the cabin with us and log on to her network."

"What now?" Parkman asked.

"No idea," Aaron said. He leaned up in the seat to read the driver's name. "Marco, do you know anyone with a MacBook laptop we could borrow for the rest of the day?"

He shook his head wide, shoulder to shoulder. "I'm sorry, I don't have friends who own such a machine. My boss has one in his office, but it's not a laptop—"

Parkman slapped the armrest on the door and sat up straighter in his seat. "Your boss has a Mac?"

"Yes, but it's a desktop computer. And I can't imagine he would lend it out to go to some cabin for the day."

"Take us to your boss."

"Can't do it. Waste of time."

"Where's your head office?"

"You're not listening. My boss is a private man. There's no way in hell that he would give you his computer, even if you gave him the couple of thousand it's worth in cash. It's his and only his. He doesn't even let his wife on it."

"You're a cab driver. We're asking you to taxi us to your boss. We'll pay the fare and then let your boss tell us that he won't let us on his system."

"No." He stared back at the two of them. "I will take you wherever you want to go, but not to my office. Either leave my cab or pick another destination."

Aaron leaned forward again, studying the identification card on the dash of the taxi. "Yellow cab. Marco Vinetti, car number 8674," Aaron said. "C'mon, Parkman. Let's go back and get Officer Kershaw to drive us to the cab company's office, where we'll talk to the boss on our own terms. I'll be sure to let him know how helpful you were as a driver for his company."

As they exited the vehicle, the driver went on about calling his boss to give him the heads up. When the doors shut, the driver sped away with the required squeal of the tires.

They half walked, half jogged back to the lawyer's office building a block and a half away. A few of the vehicles had left, but activity was still bustling around the crime scene.

Aaron saw Kershaw immediately. When they reached him, he was on his cell phone. Parkman tapped his shoulder. After a moment, Kershaw got off the call and turned to them.

"I thought you guys left."

The air was still and calm this early afternoon. After the short jog, sweat beaded up on Aaron's forehead again.

"We did leave," Parkman said. "But we need your help."

"With what?"

"We need access to a Mac, an Apple computer."

"For what?" Kershaw swiped the air at a fly buzzing too

close.

"Aaron saw something on Sarah's computer before he was attacked."

Kershaw frowned. Then adjusted his stance and faced Aaron. "I thought you were attacked outside."

"I was," Aaron said, feeling the trap closing on the lie from earlier.

"Then how did you get to see Sarah's computer? It's ruined."

"Last night. When I dropped her off after the cemetery visit."

Kershaw looked from Parkman to Aaron, then back to Parkman. Parkman kept a straight face, as did Aaron.

"What did you see?"

"An email. I think it might have information as to where Sarah is. It's a long shot, but there could be a lead. Sarah backs everything up with something called a Time Capsule —"

"I'm familiar with it."

"If I can get a MacBook Pro or any Mac for that matter, I can plug into the network back at the cabin, restore her hard drive onto the new computer, and eight hours or so later, it would be as if I have Sarah's computer back in my hand."

"And you say this message is in one of her emails?"

"Yes."

"She uses a Time Capsule." Kershaw said this more as a statement to himself. "Does she use iCloud for her email?"

Aaron nodded. "She does."

"And if you were to restore everything from the Capsule, you know her passwords to access her email?"

"I do," Aaron said. He looked at Parkman. "Where are

you going with this?"

"Follow me," Kershaw said.

He spun on his heels and started across the parking lot.

"You have a Mac?" Parkman asked.

"No, but you don't need one."

"How's that?"

"If you know her password and email address, you can log on to iCloud on any computer. It doesn't have to be a Mac. Come on, I've got a computer in the cruiser."

Chapter 13

Sarah screamed for someone to bring her a drink. Dressed in a hospital gown, her wrists and ankles were still tied to the bed. Her bladder threatened to burst half an hour ago, and her stomach ached for nourishment, but no one acknowledged her or entered the room.

A night light offered a soft glow in the darkened room, which only had one door and no windows. She had no idea if it was day or night.

All that mattered was getting untied, drinking something, using a toilet, and then hurting people until she was out of this building.

She refused to think about what Dr. Williams had said. Upon awakening, she could tell that she hadn't been violated in any other way except for Williams feeling her up before they drugged her to sleep.

Actually, she was surprised to be wearing the hospital

gown. Williams had ordered them to keep her naked. That told her something about his authority in the Amy Greg Psychiatric Hospital.

If she was under a seventy-two-hour involuntary hold, that meant someone would come to talk to her and try to assess her. They would allow the use of a bathroom. Food. Soap. Maybe a phone call.

Aaron was probably going mad after the message she left him. He would show up at the cabin, and she wouldn't be there. He'd have no idea where she had gone to meet the doctor. He wouldn't be able to reach her, and within a short time, Parkman would come, then the police would get in on it.

From what Williams said, she didn't have much time to survive this place. The only way she knew how to survive was to do it on her terms, which meant being disruptive.

She released her bladder. The warmth oozed out and puddled on the bed under her. The wetness was uncomfortable, but the pressure in her bladder ebbed, which was a relief.

They would have to change her bedsheets now. That meant untying her to take her off the bed. There'd be a new gown, possibly a shower. No one would want to do horrific things to her while she was covered in urine.

Her hunger would subside in time. It would come back stronger, but for now, she could deal with it.

Vivian's silence was more difficult. She had grown to trust her sister implicitly over the years. In the past, there were many times when Vivian was silent, and it served a purpose, but it would be so much nicer if she could just show her what would happen, so it didn't come so much of a surprise.

Surprises weren't a lot of fun.

Footsteps echoed down the corridor. They got closer. Outside her door, they stopped.

Sarah lifted her head, breath caught in her throat as she listened, staring at the door.

There was a click as the lock was disengaged, then the handle turned.

Light spilled in from the hallway. A tall man, at least six four, bald and wearing a security uniform, stepped just inside the door. He brought a hand up to his nose.

"What's that smell?" he asked.

"Bad dream. Pissed myself. Is this where I wake up? I'm still dreaming, right?"

"No, no dream. Reality. Anyway, doesn't matter. I'm supposed to take you for your shower, then new clothes and possibly breakfast. I'll have your bedsheets changed while we're away."

"And you've come to do this alone? You're not worried about me?"

He stepped closer. As he did, she saw the disfigurement on his face. A burn victim, his facial skin deformed, twisted, and melted in spots. His security guard's uniform came complete with a loaded utility belt.

He held up a small canister. "Pepper spray." He placed it back on his belt, felt around to the other side, and pulled up a small Taser. "Just in case you decide to test me, I'll be ready. Now that we know the stakes, are you ready to be placed into a wheelchair and taken for your shower?"

"A wheelchair?"

"My orders are to keep you restrained one hundred

percent of the time. Normally, there'd be two of us, but we're short-staffed. A lot of crazies in the building." He dipped his chin closer to his chest and rolled his head back and forth in short bursts in an eerie attempt to appear crazy. The skin deformity on his face only made the picture all that more alarming. He stopped rolling his head, then said, "I'll wheel the chair in and set it beside the bed. I will untie one ankle, then one wrist. You will do the rest. Understood?"

Sarah nodded.

He didn't move. After another moment, he said, "Understood?"

"Yes, for fuck's sake."

He pivoted on his heels as if he was in the military and left the room, leaving the door to the hallway open. His footfalls retreated until there was silence.

She lay her head back, stared at the ceiling, and realized something. None of Vivian's memories had surfaced to haunt her since before the doctor's appointment. What could that mean? Had Vivian retreated? Does she have that ability now that they were so close?

A noise at the door startled her. She popped her head up and looked.

A woman with a lock of white hair dangling to the side and wide, crazy eyes peeked in at her. She had to be in her sixties, but all Sarah could see was her face and that hair.

"Yes?"

"You had better watch yourself," the woman said, her voice sounding like a whiny creak of an old barn door. "There are people in here who talk."

"That's great. I talk too."

"They talk about the fourth coming and the absolution."

"The fourth coming? What happened to the second one? Or is it the third one I missed? Oh wait, that was a close encounter, wasn't it? Yes, you're right." She said in a slightly raised voice, "The fourth coming is upon us."

"The burning comes at night, and we are offered sweet release. Until dawn's early light, we awake, and we believe."

Sarah tried to take in what the woman was saying and make sense of it but couldn't. "Is it morning?"

The woman raised her head, then lowered it in quick succession. It reminded Sarah of a bobblehead on the dash of a car.

"We awake, and we believe," Sarah repeated the woman's words. "And now you believe?"

"Because of you, I believe."

Having no idea what the woman was talking about, Sarah nodded back. "Because of me."

A door slammed from somewhere down the corridor.

"Helena!" a man yelled. "What are you doing?"

The white-haired woman snapped her head to the right, and her features darkened. Then she looked back at Sarah.

"There's still time before the burning comes for you. End it, or it'll end you. The fourth—"

"Get away from that door!"

Helena disappeared, her footsteps echoing softly until they faded.

The guard from earlier pushed a wheelchair inside and stopped at the door. "Sorry about that. She's not supposed to leave her room." He kicked something on the bottom of the chair and rolled it up beside the bed. "What were you two talking about?"

"Mostly nonsense."

He moved to unstrap her left ankle. As the strap slipped free, he stepped back, out of reach if she decided to try to kick him.

He stepped up beside her left wrist and said, "Helena suffers from numerous mental maladies, but the one that angers me the most is her paruresis."

"Which is?"

"She's unable to urinate while someone is watching."

"And you routinely watch her urinate?" Sarah asked.

"In the acute ward, our job is to assist most of the patients' day-to-day functions. Some of the patients here are too unhealthy and mentally unsound to be left alone. Even to use the bathroom."

He slowly unclipped the left wrist strap and then stopped.

"There. It's loose enough that you can wiggle your way out." He stepped over to the far corner of the room by the open door. The Taser was in his hand, up and aimed in her general direction. "Undo the other two restraints. Slip slowly off the bed and sit in the chair. Once you're in the chair, strap in your ankles, then your right wrist. I will do your left one. Remember, the whole time, I have a Taser on you. Getting Tased is not pleasant, but I'll enjoy it. Start now."

Sarah did as she was told and went to work on her other restraints. Within minutes, she was in the chair, waiting for him to strap her left wrist.

It was good to get out of the wet bed. The urine had been cooling on her, making her shiver. She needed a shower and food, and then she would figure out where Cole was, deal with him and leave the building. Unless Dr. Williams returned, she would have to go after him with the police, but there was a part of her that was unsure how far that would go as he was a doctor, and they could legally commit her for observation for seventy-two hours. Unless she could trace the money or whatever it was that made him do it, she had nothing on Williams.

Fully secured to the chair, the burn victim guard pushed her out into the corridor, turned left, and started down the hall.

"What time is it?" she asked.

"Almost dinner."

"What? I thought it was breakfast. You even said breakfast."

"No, I didn't. I said dinner."

"You said breakfast."

"If I did, I meant it was your breakfast as you just woke up."

"You said breakfast."

Helena's voice echoed in her head. *The burning comes in the night ...*

The burning?

Did she mean the man pushing her wheelchair? The *burned* man pushing the chair?

Sweet release?

Was she referring to the guard? Could he be molesting the patients here? In the acute ward, where no one was sane enough to be listened to with any credibility?

Vivian's essence brushed up against her consciousness. "I'm sorry, Sarah."

The voice echoed in her head and made her jump at the intrusion.

"You okay?" the guard asked.

"Yeah."

"The only way to access Cole and see for yourself the monster he has become was to get you inside this facility," Vivian whispered.

"What?" Sarah said. "Really?"

The wheelchair slowed. They had just walked through a set of double doors. "Were you talking to me?" the guard asked.

Sarah lowered her head and shook it. "Mumbling to myself."

"He's too protected otherwise," Vivian added.

Vivian! Did you get me committed to a mental institution to meet Cole?

"You don't remember me, do you?" the guard asked. "It's the new face, isn't it?"

Another set of double doors brought them out to a set of communal showers.

"Fancy we should meet again," he said. The wheelchair stopped. He moved away.

Sarah breathed through her nose, even and regular, her head still dipped down. When he released her for the shower, she would kill him, and the burning would never come in the night ever again for any unwilling victim.

"I knew you were looking for me," he said. "I watched from afar. Saw how busy you were keeping." A shower head flicked on, the force strong. "I knew we'd meet again, Sarah. It was just a matter of time."

He started back toward her.

"Being my prisoner has its benefits. I'll take care of you just like I used to. I'll even try to make you enjoy our time together. Then you will die in the fire that will ravage this building, along with all the other crazies." He leaned down in front of her and looked up into her face. "I work the night shift. Just coming on duty, in fact. I requested everyone leave you for me to tend to. Tonight, we'll be reunited. Won't that be something?"

His burned skin didn't repulse her anymore. She wanted to grab it and tear it from his skull.

Her fingers clenched, then unclenched.

"You're upset, possibly angry. It's okay, little Sarah. I'll make you feel better tonight." He stood up and walked around behind the chair. Then he proceeded to push her under the gushing water. "Clean up, baby. Get all clean for daddy. Tonight, we party like it's 1999." He laughed, a deep rumbling chortle.

Silent fury, more than she had ever known, flowed through her veins, core, and heart, and she knew at that moment that Cole Lincoln would die a violent death and his reign of terror and rape would come to a karmic end.

She didn't suffer from any doubt on that count as the water obscured her vision of him.

"You will suffer, Cole Lincoln," she said to herself under the torrent of water. "You will suffer."

Chapter 14

AARON LEANED IN AND typed on the small keyboard of Kershaw's laptop with Parkman standing over his shoulder.

Sarah's iCloud account opened, and Aaron clicked on her inbox and opened the email reply from Rebecca. After rereading the opening lines from her, he scanned the rest of the email.

"Here, Parkman, take a look at this. Rebecca's brother is a badass. How do guys like this get through the cracks? Because he was a cop? Doesn't wash with me."

"I know how you feel about cops, but some of them are good, too," Parkman said.

"Not too many," Kershaw added. "And I'm a cop. That has got to tell you something."

After a moment, Parkman handed the computer to Kershaw. When they had read the email, Aaron signed out of Sarah's account, turned the computer off, and handed it back.

"Where's the Amy Greg Psychiatric Hospital?" Aaron asked.

"About a twenty-minute drive from here. But we can't just walk in and ask for Cole without cause."

Parkman leaned on the cruiser's roof and squinted into the afternoon sun, looking toward the building the authorities were still working in. "And how do we even know Sarah's there?"

"Where else would she be?" Aaron asked. He smacked the hood of the cruiser. "We've got nothing else to go on. No leads, no tips. All we have is someone scoping her place out last night. Two guys were watching us at the cemetery yesterday, a dead woman in Sarah's car at this office she was supposed to meet a doctor in, and still no sign of Sarah. She has to be at this Amy Greg place. Cole's there." In an exaggerated way, he shrugged and splayed his hands out to his side. "Makes sense to me. We should at least talk to Cole."

"I agree," Parkman said. "Doesn't hurt to pull Cole aside, ask a couple of innocent questions, see where he's at with this."

Kershaw scanned the men working the scene behind him. "There really is nothing else to go on." He rubbed his chin and looked down at the ground. "Aaron, you think Sarah read that email from Rebecca?" He glanced sideways at Aaron.

"No, I don't. I was the first one to read it."

"Which still doesn't work for me with the story of the attack."

"Is that what's important here? How the cabin fight played out?"

"When a woman goes missing, our person of interest is

usually the husband, the boyfriend, or the significant other in that person's life. That means you. And your cabin story doesn't add up."

Aaron raised his hands in an *I surrender* gesture. "Okay, I'll offer you a deal." He lowered his hands. "I'm suspecting that Sarah is a person of interest in that woman's death since she was found in Sarah's car." He pointed at the Dodge Charger. "Let's locate Sarah first. Get her story. Then I'll tell you my story."

"We find Sarah. I don't need your story. Nullifies the point."

"Then what are we waiting for?" Aaron said and dropped into the back seat of the cruiser.

When Parkman and Kershaw didn't move, Aaron stuck his head out. "You guys coming?"

They got in the front seat. Kershaw started the car and exited the lawyer's office parking lot.

"The deal is," Kershaw said. "We talk to Cole. Then you tell me everything. Got it?"

Aaron looked out the side window without responding. The cruiser slowed.

"Or you can talk now. I'm easy either way."

Aaron met Kershaw's eyes in the rearview mirror. "Amy Greg first."

The car sped up.

Aaron let go of the tight fist he had been holding. Sarah's life was at stake. A dead woman was found in her car. Something big was happening, and Kershaw wanted to negotiate when statements would be recorded.

It was enough to hijack the cruiser and smash it into the Amy Greg building.

He'd get inside, one way or another.
With Sarah in trouble, nothing would stop him.
Nothing.

Chapter 15

COLE THREW SARAH A towel. It hit her about the head, the ends whipping around until they rested on her shoulders.

"Dry yourself off." Cole laughed as if he'd made a joke. "I'll walk you back to your room, where you will get dressed and join the rest of the crazies for dinner."

Her hands secured to the arms of the wheelchair, Sarah shook and rocked her head until the towel slipped below her eyes.

"After a tasty mental hospital dinner," Cole said. "I've got my last set of rounds to make. Then we'll have a bit of fun before the fire."

"The fire?"

He raised his eyebrows, crossed his arms, and tilted his head to the side. "You ask about the fire. Are you not concerned about the bit of fun part?"

Wet hair spilled over Sarah's face. She pushed out her

bottom lip and blew the wisp aside. "There will be no fun," she said in a deep, cold voice. "The only fun that will be had will be mine."

Cole tilted his head to the other side. "How do you figure? You're the one tied up. You're soaked, and barely dressed, which is turning me on, by the way, and I'm in charge. I've got the weapons."

"You were saying something about a fire?"

He glared at her a moment longer, then uncrossed his arms, walked around behind the wheelchair, and started her toward the door.

"How are your parents? Amelia, right? For some reason, I can't remember your dad's name."

Sarah remained silent. It infuriated her to be in such a position, so helpless, a victim. A shudder passed through her as she clenched her hands, the restraints pressed against her wrists.

"How did you get Dr. Williams to admit me? We both know he didn't do it based on our short meeting. Those two thugs were ready and waiting."

"Oh, that part was easy." He pushed the chair through the doors and out into the corridor. "Back when I was on the force, Williams and I worked together on various cases many times. Eventually, we became friends. Golfed together and went fishing. He confided in me. A little problem that could hurt his career had popped up. A little female problem that wouldn't go away."

"So he asked you to make it go away?"

"Let's just say he dabbled with his patient when he shouldn't have, and now she wanted a payout. Pay her, and she goes away, or she tells, sues, and gets paid anyway, except the second option kills a career. It was cheaper for Williams to pay me to warn her off. A lot cheaper."

"And it didn't work, I assume."

They pushed through a set of double doors and entered the corridor that led back to Sarah's room.

"Good guess. No, it didn't work. In fact, the bitch raised the amount. Doubled it. Williams panicked. Told me he needed this issue silenced and would rather pay me than have the money extorted from him."

"Same thing, though."

There was a pause. "What?"

"Whether Williams pays her or you, the money's being spent as a result of the girl's extortion."

"But he didn't pay her."

"Whatever. What happened next?"

"I silenced the girl. In a back alley." The warmth of his breath brushed across her neck as he leaned in close to her ear. "I silenced her with my cock. She choked on it. Since then, I've been having fun and getting away with it."

"And Williams always owed you this debt."

Cole pushed the door open to Sarah's room and ushered her inside.

"He doesn't anymore. The debt has been paid. Isn't that right, Dr. Williams?"

"Yes, it is." Williams stepped out from behind the bed. "I'm debt free."

"Then why are you still here?" Sarah asked, not showing her surprise at his sudden arrival.

"I was promised a little fun with the prize. Tonight, we take turns on the legendary Sarah Roberts. In this hospital, surrounded by the institutionalized and criminally insane, we're the only normal two, and we're the ones in charge. No one will bother us. You're all alone, Sarah." Williams stepped closer, bent down, and placed his hands on his knees as he got to her level. "No one knows you're here. Before the end of the night, a fire will raze this building, and you'll die in it. I would like to think you'll focus on enjoying yourself before you die." He looked up past her to smile at Cole. "Two men at once. Your last night on Earth." His eyes found her again. "Try to enjoy it, and we'll be gentle."

"Oh, I'll enjoy myself tonight, but I won't be gentle."

Williams stood up, his face hardening. "I was afraid you'd be this way." He shrugged. "Oh well, I tried."

Sarah tested the strength of the wrist straps again, pulling up on them hard.

She didn't see Cole's right hook until it was an inch from her face.

Then she didn't see anything at all after that.

Chapter 16

KERSHAW PULLED UP OUT front of the Amy Greg Psychiatric Hospital, parked, and killed the engine.

Aaron grabbed the back door to leave but stopped when Kershaw spoke up.

"Parkman," Kershaw said. "I don't have any legal recourse here. I've got no search warrants, no paperwork, and no proof to believe Sarah is in there. And even if she is, what am I supposed to say to her?" He closed his eyes and rubbed the bridge of his nose with two fingers. "What the hell are we doing here, anyway?"

"Sarah's here," Aaron said. "I can feel it."

Parkman looked back and forth between the two of them. "This is a fishing expedition. We're going in there to ask a few questions and figure it out from there. If Sarah ever made it to this facility, people will know. If she didn't, we're about to find out."

Kershaw opened his eyes and turned to Parkman. "How will people know? What does that mean?"

"Sarah always gets results. Sometimes getting results means you have to make a little noise. If she came here looking for Cole Lincoln, you can bet there will have been some trouble."

"Hey, guys," Aaron said. "We can't learn anything in the car."

Kershaw nodded as Parkman got out, followed by Aaron. The warmth of the late afternoon on this spring day soothed Aaron as they headed for the front doors of the Amy Greg facility.

"Let me do the talking," Kershaw said. He turned back to face Aaron. "Even if we discover something you're not happy with. Deal?"

"Fine."

They hit the doors, Kershaw going through first. A reception area sat just left of the main doors. Kershaw steered that way with the two of them taking up the rear. Aaron pulled his cell phone out and flipped it to vibrate, as did Parkman.

A tall blonde woman in a vibrant yellow blouse and long black skirt exited an office, closed the door firmly, and approached them.

"How can I help you?" she asked.

"I'm Officer Nick Kershaw. My colleagues and I are looking into—"

"Is this official business?" the woman interjected.

Kershaw had a moment of uncertainty on his face. Aaron wanted to jab him in the side to prompt more talk out of him. He almost opened his mouth when Kershaw started talking again.

"Your name is?" Kershaw pulled a pad out of his breast pocket, along with a pen.

"I'm Sandra Gonzales," she said without offering a hand to shake.

Kershaw wrote it down, then pressed on. "We are looking into the disappearance of a woman named Sarah Roberts. There is reason to believe she is or will be here shortly."

"I'm not aware of her being admitted recently. But then, I don't know everyone's name." The woman sat at the reception desk, adjusting her skirt and hair. "Even if Sarah Roberts was here, you know I can't offer that kind of information without paperwork."

"She wouldn't be here as a patient."

Sandra frowned. "Then why would a missing woman show up here? Do you think she's coming to visit one of our guests?"

Kershaw exchanged a glance with Parkman, who nodded.

"She would be looking for one of your employees. A man named Cole Lincoln."

"Cole?" Sandra sat back, the chair squeaking in protest. "I'm a little confused. You have a missing woman, and yet you think she's on her way here, or already here, looking to meet with Cole?"

"That's about it," Kershaw said.

Aaron had lost patience with the dancing around. Either Sarah was here or not. He wanted to walk the length of the corridor, yelling her name.

"We have reason to believe that Sarah will be here today.

Can you confirm whether she has come in or not? Have you heard the name before now?"

"Well, Officer, without—"

"A murder has taken place. The dead woman's body was just found inside the driver's seat of Sarah Roberts's car, not far from here. Sarah has gone missing. The only recent connection to Sarah is Cole Lincoln. She was looking for him, and, as I stated earlier, we have reason to believe Sarah is here." Sandra's eyes widened noticeably as Kershaw spoke in his authoritative cop voice. "Will you confirm whether Sarah is here, or do I have to come back in an hour with twenty men and all the paperwork needed to do a little housecleaning?"

Sandra Gonzales got up and stepped to the side, pushing the chair under the desk. At first, Aaron thought she was going to run. Maybe she was a patient playing with them, and the real receptionist would be found bound and gagged in the janitor's closet.

But all Sandra did was pick up an internal paging system and hold the phone to her ear.

"Would Cole Lincoln please come to the front desk? Cole, you have visitors." She set the phone down. "I think it best that Cole handles this. He'll be here shortly. Please take a seat over there." She gestured with her fingers dangling from a limp wrist at the small collection of chairs surrounding a circular table by the main doors.

Once seated and out of earshot, Parkman turned to Kershaw. "Looks like you hit a nerve."

Kershaw nodded. "My gut tells me Sarah's here. But Sandra is right about one thing. They don't have to give me shit without proper paperwork. Since Cole is an ex-cop, and I dropped his name in connection with the disappearance of Sarah Roberts, it's a better play for them to let him handle this."

Aaron couldn't sit still. He fidgeted in the chair, bouncing both legs. "Do both of you think Sarah's here?" Aaron asked.

They nodded in unison.

"Against her will?"

Only Parkman nodded this time. "If she were here willingly, there would be more noise. Remember why she was hunting Cole in the first place. I doubt they'd be having a chat over cappuccinos in the cafeteria."

Aaron looked away and cracked his knuckles.

"When Cole comes out, I handle it," Kershaw said. He nudged Aaron's arm, who started at the intrusion. "You heard me?"

"I can't make any promises."

Kershaw got to his feet. "Get up," he said, waving his hands.

Aaron stood, his eyes locked on Kershaw's.

"Go sit in the car until we come out."

"Fuck that. You sit in the car. I'm not moving."

Parkman got to his feet behind Kershaw.

"I won't lose my job," Kershaw said, "because some hothead smacked a psychiatric security guard around. We'll handle this. That's the deal. Or I walk right now."

"Then walk," Aaron said. "This is Sarah. My Sarah. I won't sit in the fucking car."

"Last chance," Kershaw said. "No hothead stuff and I handle this, or you sit in the car."

Parkman blinked at Aaron and gave a slight shake of his

head. Sandra Gonzales watched them from the other side of the foyer.

"Okay," Aaron said. "Fuck it. Fine."

"What's fine?"

"It's your baby."

"No hothead stuff?"

"No hothead stuff."

"Shake on it."

Kershaw held his hand out. Aaron took it.

"Gentlemen," a man's voice came from behind them.

They all turned. Aaron stepped forward, but Kershaw shot a hand out and stopped him.

"I'm Officer Nick Kershaw." He let go of Aaron and held his hand out to their visitor. "And you are?"

"Dr. Lance Williams. How can I be of service to you gentlemen today?"

"We're looking to speak with Cole Lincoln."

"He's indisposed at the moment. Is there something I can help you with?"

Kershaw explained what he had told Sandra, the woman in yellow, and how they felt that Sarah Roberts might have come here looking for Cole.

"A body in her car?" Williams said. "I'm mystified. Have they ascertained a time of death yet?"

"Too early in the investigation."

There was a moment of silence. Then Williams said, "Sarah Roberts," a smirk on his face.

Kershaw frowned. "You say the name like you know her?"

"Before I say anything else, who are these two men with you?"

Parkman stepped around Kershaw and introduced himself. Aaron did the same.

"Her boyfriend?" Williams asked, keeping his attention on Aaron. "And you don't know who I am?"

"Never heard your name before," Aaron said.

"I'm Sarah's psychologist."

Aaron stepped closer. "Did she make it to her appointment this morning?"

Williams stepped back at Aaron's advance.

Kershaw shot Aaron a warning glance.

"Yes, she did," Williams said. "That's why I asked about the time of death. Was the body in the car when she met me or shortly thereafter?"

"Where is your office located?" Kershaw asked.

"On Frontier Drive. Why do you ask?"

"Frontier Drive? That's two blocks from where Sarah's car was found."

"My office used to be in another building two blocks away." Williams suddenly looked around. "Excuse me. Can we take this into an office?"

"Absolutely," Kershaw said.

They followed Williams down the corridor and into a room on the left. He closed the door and walked around to sit behind a large metal desk.

"Understandably, I can't reveal much about Sarah, but what I can say is that she's here, under my care—"

"She's here!" Aaron snapped. "For what? I demand to see her."

"Look, son, there are rules that the State of California has in place that protect the patient. What she wants to tell you is up to her, but I can only say that she's here under a seventy-two-hour hold."

"Hold for what?" Aaron said, his thighs pressing on the back of the desk.

"That's enough," Kershaw stepped in beside Aaron.

"No, it's okay." Williams raised a hand for calm. "I understand. You're emotionally attached to her. I can tell you that she's okay right now. At this moment, she's participating in a group therapy session." He cleared his throat. "I might be able to pull some strings and give you a quick visit tomorrow if you were to return."

"Why is she here?" Parkman asked.

"She came to me for help. Sarah needs more help than she would receive in one-hour sessions at my office. I don't commit people for observation lightly. Under California law, she was allowed one phone call. You know, to let people close to her know where she is. I'm sorry that you weren't her chosen call."

Aaron moved Kershaw aside, making it clear he wasn't to stand in front of him again. "And how does it help Sarah that the one person Sarah has an issue with is Cole Lincoln, a guard at this hospital? Or was that the plan? To get them together? Are you helping Sarah or working for Cole?"

"Now, wait just one minute," Williams said as he shot up from behind the desk. "What exactly are you insinuating? Are you accusing me of something, young man?"

"I think that's enough," Kershaw interrupted.

"I've been a psychologist in the State of California for over two decades. When I say a patient needs to be held for a seventy-two-hour observation, I have deemed that they appear to be a danger to themselves or others. This is not a criminal distinction. Within a couple of days, she will be free to go. Whether or not she has a history with a staff member has not come up during her therapy sessions."

Then it donned on Aaron that this was exactly where Sarah wanted to be. She probably met with Williams and convinced him to commit her. Now, inside these walls, Sarah will finally get to Cole. Even if it wasn't Sarah consciously, then Vivian had something to do with it. Either way, standing here and trying to get answers from Williams could thwart anything Sarah had set in motion, which would only upset her. They had probably gone too far already.

Aaron backed up and raised his hands. "It's okay," he said. "I'll leave. I'm sorry. I don't know what came over me." The room grew silent. Everyone stared at him. "We came to learn of her whereabouts. We've found her in your care. Everything is fine now." Aaron smiled wide as he reached the door to the office.

"It's not fine yet," Kershaw said. "An investigation will have to be held into where and when Sarah was committed and how a body found its way into Sarah's car."

Aaron stayed near the door. Parkman caught his eye and frowned. With a jerk of his head, Aaron got Parkman to follow him out into the corridor. The entrance to the office closed, leaving Kershaw and Williams alone in the room.

"What's with the about-face?" Parkman asked.

Aaron checked to make sure the woman in yellow wasn't close by. Then he leaned in close to Parkman. "How do we not know that this has been Sarah's plan the whole time?"

"What are you thinking?" Parkman asked.

"She wanted to locate Cole. Now she has. Not only has she found him, but she also couldn't just wait for him outside until he got off shift and walked to his car. There are stalking laws and harassment laws against that sort of thing. Why not commit herself for seventy-two hours? Spend three days in an asylum, scoping him out, learning his ways, getting to know him. Here we are, about to fuck that up for her when we both know Sarah can handle herself. She's got Vivian, too." He slapped Parkman's arm. "We must learn to step aside and only come when she calls for us."

Parkman looked away. He seemed to be thinking about it. "Makes sense. But something still doesn't add up."

"What's that?"

"How do you explain the body in her car? Murder doesn't fit into that picture. And if something happened where the murder was justified, Sarah wouldn't leave the body in her car. The body was left on purpose to be found, and she's going to have to explain it. Or someone else will."

"Shit. You're right. Then what's really going on?"

Parkman shrugged. "No idea. That's why we're here. At least we know Sarah's here, and so is Cole. Maybe this'll wrap up faster than we anticipated."

The office door opened. Kershaw stepped out and started down the corridor toward the front doors.

"C'mon, guys," he said over his shoulder.

Aaron and Parkman fell in step behind him. When they were outside, Kershaw pulled up short of his car and turned around. For a second, Aaron thought he would blast him for being aggressive back there, but he didn't. He said something altogether worse.

"Sarah's in trouble. They're holding her against her will, and we have to get her out of here."

"What?" Parkman stammered. "What did Williams say?"

"He's hiding something and enjoying it. I've seen the

gleam in his eye in a thousand assholes on the street. He's in charge, protected by patient confidentiality. No one will dare challenge him. Without proper papers, no one will see Sarah for another two days. She's alone in that asylum with Williams running the show and that Cole guy on shift right now." Kershaw shook his head. "Something stinks. Even after I told him we found a body in Sarah's car, his surprised act was see-through." Kershaw put a hand on Aaron's shoulder. "I'm sorry, Aaron. Let's head back to the station and see what we can do about this. Even if we can't get Sarah out of here for the next two days, I'll at least get them to grant me a visitation in light of the murdered woman in her car. We have to see that she's okay. We just have to because I don't think she is. Something tells me she's in a lot of trouble."

Kershaw spun on his heels, and half walked, half ran for the car.

"If he's right," Aaron said, "there goes my theory of her wanting to be here."

"It was only a theory," Parkman added.

Once they were all in Kershaw's car, he squealed the tires on the way out of the parking lot.

When Aaron looked back at the doors they had just exited, Dr. Williams stood there, watching them leave.

It looked like Williams was smiling.

Chapter 17

THE SCENT OF FOOD wafting down the corridor from the dining area made her stomach ache. She hadn't eaten since being brought in.

Cole leaned down and whispered, "Your hands are secured to the wheelchair and won't be untied. I'll be feeding you."

He pushed her chair toward the dining area.

"What am I supposed to have?" Sarah asked.

"Whatever's cooking."

"No, not food, condition. What psychosis have you fabricated to get me here? I must be badass to be locked to a chair and a bed with no one saying anything about it."

"Your diagnosis is the Macdonald Triad."

"What's that?"

They entered an area filled with tables. Patients in various levels of dress and cleanliness meandered through the tables, plates of food in their hands. Someone laughed high and loud, the kind heard at a circus. Another person to Sarah's right grunted.

"The Macdonald Triad is also called the triad of sociopathy. Fancy words for a set of three behavioral characteristics with violent tendencies. Basically, you're a predator who commits serial offenses. You destroyed your cabin, too."

She turned and glared at him. "I did what?"

"You destroyed your cabin. Then killed that receptionist in Williams's office. With your history, which has been documented in the media for years, it will be an easy sell."

"Why kill the woman? Why wreck the cabin? Only to justify why you locked me up? Or to cover up more of yours and Williams's indiscretions?"

"Beef stroganoff and steamed carrots are on the menu tonight," he said, ignoring her questions. "You'll enjoy the beef, Sarah. Think of this as your last meal."

He pushed her chair into a vacant corner by the window. He left her and started toward the food trays. Outside, the sun was an hour away from disappearing, and still nothing from Vivian.

Where are you? she asked. *Could use a little help here.*

A woman pivoted to look at Sarah. She snapped her head Sarah's way so fast that her body shook with the effort. Then the woman, dressed in a drab brown top and too-short shorts, shot to her feet.

Sarah glanced at Cole, who hadn't noticed the woman's odd behavior. When she looked back, the woman was already walking toward Sarah. Sarah jerked her hands up in defense, but the restraints held fast. The woman's mouth moved, eyebrows twitched, and her hands clenched and unclenched as she strode toward Sarah.

Ten feet from the wheelchair, the woman burst into a run and dove at Sarah. Out of reflex, Sarah flinched and shoved her body to the side of the chair but couldn't get too far.

The woman smashed into the wall just behind the wheelchair, slamming her fists into the eggshell white paint, ranting gibberish.

"Code one!" a man yelled from somewhere in the room.

Then Cole was on the crazy woman, attempting to subdue her arms without success as she flailed at the wall. Three other men show up and land on the woman. A needle was produced, and then they got her turned over, pushing her into the chair's wheelbase. Moments later, they took the woman away as she kicked and screamed.

Cole breathed deep, hitched up his pants, and turned to Sarah.

"Code one was for the schizophrenic patients who scream and punch the walls. Katy often hears voices and sees monsters that aren't there." Cole offered Sarah a sardonic smile. "I would too if my uncle locked me in a basement cage for twelve years and raped me daily until nothing was left inside but fear, anger, and a lovely schizoaffective disorder. Well, almost nothing left inside, there's still a little something in Katy for me." He leaned down and whispered, "But let's keep that between us."

He left Sarah in the chair, shaken from lack of food and the anger that almost felt like it was consuming her.

Do I always have to deal with human scum? I seem to be haunted by them.

But Sarah knew the answer. She would spend the rest of

her days, however many she had left, dealing with men like Cole because she could fight back. Men like Cole were her prey. She was a predator, after all. And she was here hunting Cole Lincoln and had added Dr. Williams to her list.

Cole brought over a small plate of food, whisked a chair around in front of Sarah, and stuck a fork full of moist beef in Sarah's face. Taking anything from the sick man in front of her was the last thing she ever thought she could do, but nourishment offered a better chance at leaving this building. She had to eat. She opened her mouth. He hesitated, staring inside at her tongue, her throat. She almost closed it again, but the fork moved forward, and she accepted the food.

"The Macdonald Triad describes an obsession with fire setting, which you will do tonight. It also covers enuresis, or bedwetting, which you already did on your own. I have to thank you for that." He smiled that horrid grin of his as he stirred her food and offered up more. "According to Dr. Williams, fire setting is a release of aggression. You, Sarah Roberts, seem quite aggressive."

As she listened to Cole rant about her supposed conditions, she ate and thought of escape. Before the fire broke out in the hospital, she tried to save as many people as possible. But how if she couldn't even save herself?

"After dinner," Cole continued, "everyone will go for closure group to see if they met their daily goals. You won't be joining them. That's the time when you'll be investigating me."

"Huh?"

"That's right. You'll have stored all my files and patient complaint forms in your room. How you did it will remain a mystery for most, but then they'll locate my key card on your person when the fire marshal conducts his investigation."

The stroganoff was done, and the carrots tasted horrible.

"I'm done eating."

Cole set the plate aside and looked around the room. No one was close enough to hear them, and even if they were, how much would it matter?

Helena, the white-haired woman from earlier, who spoke of the burning coming in the night, stared at Sarah from the other side of the room.

The burning, the burning ...

She looked at Cole's face as he spoke, not hearing him. The burn marks on his face. *The burning. Coming in the night. Sweet release.* Now Cole wanted to burn the building down with all the patient files in Sarah's room.

It's a cleansing.

Vivian.

A cleansing for Lance Williams and Cole Lincoln. And who better to be blamed for the cleansing but Sarah Roberts, an old family friend who has been obsessed with Cole since he was her babysitter all those years ago?

"By nine tonight, we'll offer everyone their night meds," Cole continued. "There will be Seroquel and Gabitril for sleep, and for depression, we'll be offering Abilify. At eleven tonight, when everyone is drugged and falling into a psychotic dream-filled sleep, you'll be preparing your masterpiece. A nurse will call for lights out, and the fire will start. How does that sound?"

"Wonderful." It was Sarah's turn to smile. Vivian was back. A couple of thoughts, accompanied by images, came to Sarah in rapid succession. "But you forgot one thing," she added.

"What's that?" Cole had a smug look on his face like he was waiting for the punch line of a joke. "I haven't forgotten anything. This plan existed before you began your little search for me. That woman who died took part in the search for you. She knew too much. Her body was found in your car. How the hell do you think you will ever walk away from here—"

"Cole," a man said.

Dr. Williams had walked up behind him.

"What?"

"A cop and two others were just here looking for Sarah."

"And? What did they want?"

"To see her." He pointed at Sarah. "To talk to her. They found the body in Sarah's car. The cop might become a problem."

Cole shook his head. "No, he won't. It's late. The fireworks are set to start in a few hours. He can't get the necessary warrants in that time. Who were the other two men?"

"Her boyfriend, Aaron, and a friend, a man who only gave the name Parkman."

A warmth coursed through her. They were here. They knew where she was. Her men. Her lover. How they found her so fast was a miracle, but it made her feel loved. She would get out of this, deal with Cole and Williams, and be home for breakfast.

"Too bad they missed out." Cole turned back to Sarah. "We'll be the last two sane men you ever see." He got up, set the dinner plate on a table, and then turned to Williams. "Don't worry about them. Stay focused. Come find me after the closure group session is over. We get started as everyone heads to bed. I've got final rounds to make after I wheel her back to her room. I'll leave you to finish the preparations."

Williams patted Cole on the shoulder and stepped away with what Sarah thought was a tight, worried look on his face.

Cole grabbed the handles of the wheelchair and pushed Sarah from the dining room toward the corridor that led back to her room.

"Oh, yeah, you were saying I missed something," Cole said.

Vivian's thoughts were clear in Sarah's head. She knew what to do but wasn't sure of the outcome.

"The fire will be small and contained. Most of what you are planning will not happen." The chair slowed momentarily, then picked up again. Low enough that only he could hear, she said, "Your last breath will be because I took it."

When they got to her room, he shoved her inside and slammed the door closed behind her without another word.

She smiled as it all came clear.

And she waited as any good hunter would.

Chapter 18

With no clock on the wall, Sarah could not know how long she sat in the wheelchair, waiting for Williams or Lincoln to show up. Her bladder ached, her throat was dry, mild images of Vivian's past flitted through her mind, and she had an itch. But none of that bothered her anymore. She had learned a long time ago some things were more important than taking a piss or scratching an itch.

Over and over, she thought about what Vivian had told her, examining it from all angles. More importantly, this time, Vivian had *shown* her some of what was going to happen. Like a future déjà vu. As if she had been there, done that, but it hadn't happened yet.

There were uncertainties, but that didn't sway Sarah's belief that this would end in her favor. What was of utmost importance was that the files didn't burn. Somewhere inside those files were the complaints of several patients.

Complaints about Cole's conduct.

It appeared Cole had been assaulting women for more than fifteen years and getting away with it by putting himself in positions where his integrity would never be questioned. Who would believe the word of a psych patient, especially one who invents voices and sees monsters?

Sarah scanned the boxes from her chair. They were piled six high in the far corner of her room. With the single bulb— it had to be a sixty-watt—dangling over the bed, there was just enough light in the back corner to see where a black marker had been used to mark the boxes with dates. Some of them went back four and five years.

If they all held truths that Cole wanted to be destroyed, how come there were boxes dated that far back? Couldn't someone have put it together by now? Or was this an old-boys club where doctors like Lance Williams help cover up for men like Cole?

Sarah understood why Vivian directed her to go to Dr. Williams now. It was the only way to get this deep into Cole's world. And with him about to burn whatever evidence he was collecting, along with burning her too, and have the blame fall on Sarah, getting out of this was still in question.

Vivian's thoughts and messages gave her a little insight, but not enough to pull off an escape. She would need help. But from where? And when?

Suddenly the uncertainties were ominous.

She was tied to a chair with straps that were impossible for her to get out of. If they moved her to the bed, she would be strapped down there, too.

Maybe outside help would come in time?

The door clicked. It opened.

Dr. Williams stepped inside, stuck his head back out to look up and down the hallway, then closed the door and locked it. He turned to face her, held up the key he locked the door with, smiled wide, then slipped it inside his coat pocket.

"Everything's set," he said as he walked across the room toward the boxes. There, he produced a keycard, also holding it up for Sarah to see. "This is the key that allows access to the room that held these files." He set it on top of the nearest box and turned back to face her. "Somehow you got the key," he said, his tone sarcastic, "stole these boxes, and one by one, for all fifteen of them, brought them to your room to review." He shrugged. "Who knows what you were thinking? That's something for the investigators to figure out." He moved closer to her chair. "Of course, I will help with the investigation, steering them where they need to go. My diagnosis has already been written and submitted." He stopped in front of her, his knees almost touching hers. "You're certifiable. A psychopath and a pyromaniac who gets off on setting fires. Your destruction of this wing of the Amy Greg Psychiatric Hospital was a plan that, even in your deluded consciousness, you were able to pull off. After all, you've wanted to kill Cole Lincoln for some time. You waited until he was on shift—"

"Cut the bullshit," Sarah snapped.

He stopped, his mouth hanging open.

"Ego much?" she said. "I get it. You've got a foolproof plan. You're both geniuses. The both of you have raped and assaulted your victims for years and gotten away with it, and now you plan to destroy whatever's in those boxes and me, along with them, to keep getting away with it. All right, already. You both talk too much. Get on with it. Start the show so I can finish this and go home for dinner. I'm hungry. And I'll need a hot bath after dealing with the likes of you."

Williams's mouth closed. For a prolonged time, he stared down at her.

"You really are crazy." The laugh that emitted from him was forced, strained. "Home for dinner? That's something. I'd like to see how you'll pull that off."

She braced for a blow to the head or something equally painful, but it didn't come. Instead, Williams moved to the boxes and examined them until he came to one labeled with zeros. After moving a few aside, he lifted the lid off the zeroed box and produced a red gas can. When he turned back to face her, the dim light in the room cast a dark shadow on his features, making his grin one of absolute madness.

He looked like a demented doctor from an eighties horror movie, the gas can his talisman.

The first pangs of fear flipped her stomach. "Seems like you thought of everything." She kept her face pensive, deadpan.

He unscrewed the cap on the large gas can and took a whiff of the contents, drawing his head back in a jerking motion.

"Whew, what a smell. Do you know what that smells like?"

"Sure. But I have a feeling you'll tell me anyway."

"It smells of burning skin and death. Your death."

"I suggest you smell it again. Then again. Maybe the fumes will repair what's wrong inside your twisted head."

"Insult me, mock me, enjoy your false bravado. That's all you've got. An empty shell of a woman, chasing ghosts from the past." He set the gas can down by his feet. "A coping mechanism." His mouth sagged until his face formed a moue, almost as if he was pouting for her. "I understand. Facing certain death must have its drawbacks."

"Ask yourself. The reason the door on my cabin was locked wasn't to protect me at night. It's to protect you from me."

"Cute." He slipped out of his doctor's jacket and retrieved the room key and a Bic lighter from the right pocket. He tossed the jacket on the boxes and set the key and lighter on the floor by the gas can. Then he proceeded to undo the belt from his jeans and moved forward.

"You must be strapped back onto your bed, but I can't use meds. If you're doped up and only partially burned, and they do a toxicology report as part of the autopsy, there will be questions about how you were successful in burning this ward while on meds. That leaves me with this belt. I will use it for your neck as I remove you from the chair. Try anything, and I will strangle you, then burn you. Understand?"

Sarah glared at him, a muscle under her right eye twitching.

Where's Cole? He's the one I want.

"Understand?" Williams asked again in a harsher voice.

Sarah nodded. "I get it."

Williams stepped behind her and lowered the belt around her throat. He pulled the end inside the buckle until it was taut. As he did, Sarah tried to flare her neck out to give her room to breathe later if he pulled it too tight, but it didn't work. During her recent training with Aaron and hand-to-hand combat lessons, her body had grown tight, muscles cut. Her neck was surrounded by a thin layer of fat, not enough to make a difference.

The grip of the belt made the air escaping her throat raspy. He loosened it some, but not enough for her to breathe normally.

"I will do one hand at a time," he said.

He undid her right hand first. Then, as she lifted it from the chair's arm, free of restraints, the belt tightened to where breathing stopped.

"Place it on the bed," he demanded. "Now!"

Eyes bulging, lungs yearning, Sarah shot her arm out, close enough for him to secure her wrist to the bed's restraints. The pressure in her head increased as he worked one-handed on securing her. Her mouth opened and closed like a landed fish, unable to dispel or grab air. Then, gratefully, the wrist restraint on the bed gripped her skin, and the belt around her neck loosened simultaneously. She gulped air in waves, her vision clearing.

"Okay, okay," Sarah said. "Take it easy on the belt on this one."

"Can't do that," Williams said as he began to undo Sarah's left hand from the chair. "I've got to completely release you from the chair now, legs and all. You will only have your right arm secured to the bed, your stronger arm, but it still offers you a fighting chance." Her left wrist popped free. He knelt in front of her and placed a hand on the ankle cuffs as he glanced up, meeting her eyes. "I have to do this alone. If you try anything, all I have to do is back away to be out of reach. But if you test me, I will break your arms and try again. Believe me when I say I will do it. I'll end up having to use meds to sedate you. I'll make sure your body is in the center of the fire so you burn so much not even dental records will help them identify you. Am I getting to you in there?"

Almost imperceptibly, Sarah nodded. Her breathing was deep but back under control.

"Good. Now, gently, I will release your ankles. I am going to walk around behind you and hold the belt, but this time I won't cut off your breathing if you do as I tell you. Cool?"

Watching her eyes, Williams pulled the ankle restraints off and backed away from Sarah. He walked behind her and gripped the belt.

"Get up from the chair slowly and lie on the bed on your back. Do it now."

As much as she wanted to do something, to fight, there was no play here. With one arm bound and a belt around her neck, she was vulnerable to his whim. Without wanting to startle him, Sarah eased up and out of the chair, using her left hand to push up on the armrest as her legs were still weak and unsure.

She leaned into the oversized gurney and rolled onto her back. The strap around her right wrist was attached to the bed by a six-link chain. The chain appeared to have been added as an afterthought. Leaving her legs bent at the knee, feet flat, she set her left wrist in place to be bound, still thinking there was no other play here.

The entire time the belt around her neck remained loose enough to breathe without an issue.

"Well done," Williams said.

He clipped the strap around her left wrist and secured it. Now both arms were bound to the bed, but her legs remained free. He released his grip on the belt around her neck but left it dangling there. She eased up toward the end of the bed, so her head dipped off the edge to avoid the uncomfortable digging of the belt in the back of her neck.

"You just helped kill yourself," Williams said.

He came into view. She frowned at him. "How's that?" she asked.

He walked to the end of the bed and looked up at her. She closed her knees, feeling naked in nothing but the robe-like hospital wear and panties.

Without another word, he jumped up on the end of the bed, ripped her knees apart, and shoved her feet off the edge, forcing them down by pushing on her thighs.

She yelped at the sudden movement and pain that shot through her legs as both hands reflexively yanked their binds to the ends of the six-link chains.

He pulled forward and dropped between her legs, pushing down on her groin as he fumbled with the clasp on his jeans.

"We're going for one more round before I burn you, bitch."

She shouted at him and bucked her hips, but it was no use. She had no leverage with her legs forced off the edge of the bed on each side, her feet almost touching the floor, and her hands secured and useless above her head.

She felt his skin on her inner thighs. Bile rose in her throat, and a crazy thought entered her mind that this moment would add to the other horrific memories that haunt her. That's all this was: another memory to add to the collection.

But that was acquiescence. That was giving up.

And Sarah never gave up.

He was pushing on her panties, trying to rip them from her.

She heard a tearing of material, and her mind slipped out. And into gear. Not fourth gear; overdrive.

She lifted her head and said, "Give it to me, baby."

He snapped his face toward her and stopped moving. His left arm shoved down between their joined pelvises where he was attempting to gain entry.

And then Sarah made her move.

Chapter 19

AARON COULDN'T TAKE IT anymore. The waiting, the inaction, the inability for anyone to do anything without someone else authorizing it. He learned a long time ago, when his sister Joanne went missing in Toronto, that the police really do have their hands tied. Through Sarah, he was also learning to let it go and not judge them as harshly as he had in the past. It wasn't their fault. They had a job to do, a system to uphold, and accountability to a system. It was almost impossible to remain inside the boundaries without lawyers present at every turn.

But Aaron didn't have those constraints. He could do what he wanted when he wanted. His only accountability was to maintain standards that kept him out of jail. But on nights like this, with his patience thinning, he found that more and more difficult.

Since he had ridden in with Kershaw and Parkman, he

had no car at the police station and couldn't steal one.

Call a cab? No, they'd trace it and follow him.

Ask for a ride back to his car. They'd follow him.

Stealing a police car as Sarah had done in the past wouldn't work. Unlike Sarah, he'd get arrested, which meant he couldn't help Sarah when and if she needed him.

Then an idea occurred to him. He excused himself, telling Parkman he was headed to the restroom.

"I'll be back in ten to fifteen minutes."

Parkman nodded, but Aaron felt Parkman's eyes on him the whole way down the police headquarters corridor.

As he walked past the front desk, he snatched a couple of Officer Nick Kershaw's business cards so he'd have his number when he needed it.

Once outside, Aaron broke into a run.

"Hey!" someone yelled from behind him.

His feet smacked the pavement as he stopped and turned back.

Parkman stood in the doorway, his arms crossed.

"Where're you headed?" he asked.

"To get Sarah."

After a moment of silence between them, Parkman unfolded his arms, opened the door to go back inside, then said loud enough for Aaron to hear, "Go get her, and good luck."

Aaron walked backward until Parkman disappeared inside, then he pivoted and bolted down the street. What he had planned was a long shot, but he had to try. Whether Sarah was in that mental hospital willingly or not, he needed to talk to her to find out what was going on.

If his plan worked, he would be offered access to the

Amy Greg Psychiatric Hospital without resistance.

If his plan worked.

He ran harder.

Chapter 20

OFF BALANCE, HIS ARM still plunged between their groins, Williams leaned slightly to Sarah's left. The pressure that held her right leg off the edge of the bed had decreased.

"I said, give it to me!" Sarah shouted.

Then, before he realized his mistake in leaning off to one side, Sarah bent her right leg, forced the thigh up, and shoved her knee toward Williams.

He caught the movement in his peripheral vision and pulled his hand free to block her leg, but it was too late. Her knee came in fast, connected weakly with his shoulder, bounced off, then came in again. One-handed, he fumbled for purchase but missed her leg as Sarah pulled it away, aimed higher, and shouted as she brought it in again.

This time her knee smacked Williams in the left ear, knocking his head to the side. A grunt of pain escaped his lips as he used his right hand to balance himself on top of her.

Otherwise, he would have fallen off the side.

Not missing a beat, when Williams moved to grab Sarah's leg with both hands, she brought her left one up and into action. Both legs encircled his waist, and she locked her ankles over his lower back.

She ground her teeth, fisted her hands, and moaned as she caught him in a scissor hold, her legs tightening with each second. He pounded at her thighs as best he could, but she ignored it. After another intake of breath, she held it and squeezed tighter.

Dr. Williams screamed under the pressure. Not in great physical shape, he had grown flabby around the waist due to glycemic stress. Without any serious muscular resistance from him, Sarah continued to squeeze his abdomen, lifting him up off the table as she flexed her stomach until he was almost hovering above her.

Then, in a lightning-quick move, she unlocked her legs, brought the left one around in front of him before the dazed Williams could respond, and wrapped the back of her knee around his neck. With the leg bent around his neck, she was able to crane his head to the side at a forty-five-degree angle as she squeezed.

He made inhuman sounds, moans, and internal cries as she forced his head down, hoping the force would crack something in his neck.

Pushed by the memories that haunted her, driven by what he had been about to do to her, and offered a chance to save future victims, Sarah added a level of fury into the force around Williams's neck until his head was inverted, dangling by the side of the bed, the rest of his body following.

She slipped her right leg under him to keep him on the

bed as his body began to slip too far to her left, but it was too late.

When her leg had wrapped around Williams's head and pushed him sideways, gravity did the rest, and the inevitable happened. Williams's body, the fight knocked out of him, slipped off her bed and hit the floor. In order to not lose her advantage or his head, Sarah tightened her leg with every ounce of strength left in it, but the man's overweight body hit the floor and yanked the head out of her grasp.

And just like that, the fight was over. Williams was on the floor, and Sarah was still on the bed, wrists tied, with nothing to defend herself but her legs. He would be more cautious and prepared the next time he approached her. He would secure her legs so nothing like that would ever happen again.

She had made a mistake by trying to strangle him or break his neck using her leg instead of an arm. Had she kept him in the scissors hold where he couldn't breathe too well, he would've passed out eventually.

But regrets weren't how she made it out of jams time and time again. How she did it was forward-thinking and a little help from the other side.

Anything, Vivian?

She turned to look for him. Williams was crawling away from her, his head dangling to the side at a weird angle. Maybe she did hurt him. Maybe she snapped something or pulled a muscle. She could only hope.

Then it occurred to her what he was doing.

He was crawling toward the room key and the lighter, which sat beside the gas can.

"How was your childhood?" she asked.

Was there anything she could do to stall him?

Think, Sarah. Dammit!

"Your father beat you?"

She pulled on her cuffs, yanking the chain to the end, and tilted her head back to examine them.

"When you were younger, did you have a boyfriend? Is that why you're fixated on raping women because you could only get it up when you're forcing it?"

Instigating him wouldn't help, but she couldn't stop him and wasn't about to beg him to stop. All she knew how to do was instigate.

"I get it. That's why you force yourself on women. Because you're a coward. A fucking coward who couldn't measure up to his father and never amounted to anything in your mother's eyes."

She kicked the bed. There had to be a way out of this.

"You're wrong," Williams muttered from the pile of boxes.

He had made it across the floor and was now sitting up against the boxes, gas can in one hand, lighter in the other. The room's key reflected the single lightbulb five feet from him.

He had made up his mind. A determination flared in his eyes, and his forehead shined where fine beads of sweat had emerged.

"I'm not wrong," she said. "Rape is wrong. You do it because you're weak. You're a coward, a rapist, and a murderer. You're an asshole, and most of all, you don't belong here anymore."

He frowned as if what she said was some big puzzle. "Belong where?"

"Here, on this plane."

"We're not on a plane." He wiped his face. "We're in a mental hospital, and by the sounds of it, we're right where you're supposed to be."

"Let me assure you, we're on a plane. The other side is another plane of existence, and that's where you're headed next."

"We're all headed there eventually."

He began to undo the cap of the gas can.

"You're going to the other side a hell of a lot faster than the rest of us," Sarah said, "where you'll have to answer for what you've done down here."

"Whatever. I'm an atheist. There is no other side. When I leave here, I'll be dust or worm food. Whichever doesn't matter to me, as I'll be gone."

He tossed the cap to the side, turned away from her, and started to get up off the floor.

Sarah pulled herself up until her head dangled completely off the end of the bed. Then she planted both feet, lifted her hips, took a deep breath, and pushed off. She curled her legs up toward her head, lifted her lower back off the bed, and kept the momentum going forward as the rest of her spine came away from the surface of the bed.

Then her feet were over her head. Next came her knees, and finally, crumpled up, her weight drove her the rest of the way over. Her backward somersault brought her off the bed, her feet landing flat on the cool floor at the head of her bed. During the flip, her wrists spun the six-link chain in a small circle, twisting it some, but not enough to cause a problem.

Williams was on his feet, his back to her, his neck still craned to the side. He tilted the gas can and let its contents spill from the opening. It splashed on the boxes, the thick scent reaching Sarah's nose immediately, making her want to cough.

She gripped the edge of the bed and tried to push as if it was on wheels, but it didn't move. The brakes were easy to flip up and off on the two wheels on her side of the bed, but she couldn't reach the other two.

Williams set the gas can down and turned to her.

"Instead of burning the witch at the stake—" he stopped talking when he saw her standing at the head of the bed. "Hey, how did you …?"

Sarah pushed down, forcing the other end of the bed to lift. Then she spun the bed toward him.

Williams dropped so fast that it looked like he'd collapsed at the waist. He rose just as fast, the lighter in his hand, thumb on the spin wheel.

He smiled wide, his teeth showing. "I see you'd prefer we both die in here."

She ran, pushing the end of the bed toward him.

He flicked the lighter, and a flame appeared. Without attempting to move out of the way, Williams set the lighter to the gas-soaked boxes and braced for impact.

As the bed's metal frame contacted Williams's waist, the gas ignited in a huge ball of fire, forcing Sarah back with the immediate and intense wall of flame and heat.

She fell on her ass hard, the bed above protecting her from the immediacy of the flames to some degree. Her wrists yanked back in their restraints, twisting, making her screech at the sudden pain.

Oxygen was sucked up, and the initial rise of the flames decreased to a small fire as the dry cardboard of the boxes caught.

As she got to her feet, she scrunched up a corner of the bedsheets and covered her nose to breathe. The partially burned Williams was on the floor, crawling away from the rising flames. She spun the bed toward him, keeping the end with the two locked wheels off the floor. Then she shoved it forward. The bed vibrated violently when it connected with Williams.

Without wasting time, she pushed down so the bed would rise again, spun it out of the way, and came around so she could stand beside him. He was bleeding from the side of his face and forehead area. His shoulders showed signs of being singed by the sudden burst of flames, and a large part of his hair, beard, and mustache curled up where the fire burned it back.

He lifted his head to look up at her, the side of his face reddened by heat. Fury and hatred oozed off him in waves. The look of disgust on his features made her grin back at him, even though she had the urge to cough. He shoved his hand outward as if he threw something and then laughed.

"What's so funny?" Sarah asked.

"We're both going to die," he said, then coughed.

"I agree. Just not on the same day. I'm sure you will die today, but I'll make it a few more years."

"No," he said, looking up at her again. "You die today, too. I just threw the room key out under the door. It's somewhere in the hallway now. Good luck getting out of here alive."

She lifted her foot and brought her heel down on his cheek, slamming his face into the floor and the wicked grin from his features.

His eyes rolled up in his head, and he slumped down like a wind-up toy all out of the wind-up.

She coughed, then drove her foot into his face once more, harder, for good measure. She couldn't allow Dr. Williams to become a problem when she left this building.

When she turned to look at the spot where the room key had been earlier, it was gone. A quick scan of the floor revealed no key.

He hadn't lied. That arm thrust must have been the key to leaving the room.

She was locked inside with the unconscious and partially burned doctor.

And the fire was building with intensity across the wall of boxes at the back of her room, with no way to quell the flames.

Chapter 21

AARON MADE IT TO the local hospital within fifteen minutes of leaving the police station. The building stood three stories high with a brick tower that displayed a large H on it. From his position on the east side of the building, Aaron saw a helicopter parked on the roof near the brick tower.

The area seemed calm as the evening wore on, the parking lot half full. He located the emergency doors and stayed to the side, searching for the ambulance entrance. Around one corner and past another set of double doors brought him to a restricted area for emergency personnel only.

He carefully pushed open the door, grateful he didn't need a keycard. No sirens or buzzers sounded. He breathed a sigh and continued forward.

Footsteps approached.

He hopped behind a wall in a corridor that led to a

restroom and flattened himself against it until the person walked far enough away. Then he stepped back into the main hall and started toward the door that led to the ambulances.

From the moment he entered the hospital until he stepped up beside one of the parked ambulances, it couldn't have been more than two minutes.

Voices moved closer. He ducked down as two men approached, talking about a football game. He lowered himself under the edge of the ambulance.

A few seconds later, the men materialized beside the vehicle and kept walking. They entered the hospital and disappeared behind the sliding doors.

Aaron rolled out and got to his feet. With one more look around to ensure no one was watching, he opened the ambulance door and checked for keys.

They were there, dangling from the ignition.

Perfect!

He opened the door wider to be able to hop in when a voice stopped him.

"Excuse me? What are you doing there?"

Aaron froze. Steal the ambulance anyway? Knock the guy out and steal the ambulance? They'd have the police looking for him in record time. But what other options did he have?

He contorted his face into a mask of grief and sadness, then turned to address the man who interrupted him. It was one of the ambulance drivers.

"Please," he pleaded, tears coming to his eyes. "There's been an accident—" His voice caught, and he stifled a cry. "My wife … I need an ambulance."

While he talked, the ambulance driver's partner stepped

out to join him.

"You're not supposed to be in this area, sir," the first attendant said.

"I don't have a cell phone. I couldn't call it in." He wiped at his eyes. "There's been a horrific accident."

The paramedics looked at each other and then back at Aaron. In a second, he would abort this plan, drop the both of them, and steal the ambulance anyway if they didn't buy what he was selling.

"We didn't get a call. No one has dispatched any ambulances to an accident—"

Losing some of the grief look, Aaron turned it to anger, which seemed easier. "You didn't get the call," he shouted. "Because I don't have my cell. And while we stand here bickering, my wife …" He stopped and lowered his head. "If she dies, it's on you two."

The second guy walked around to the passenger side of the vehicle, opened the door, and grabbed the radio. He proceeded to call in and see if there were any accident scenes being reported.

Before he received a response, Aaron pulled Kershaw's business card out and handed it over to the first guy.

"Ask Kershaw. He's the one who sent me up here from the police station."

The guy examined the card, then looked up at Aaron. "Okay, I'll call Kershaw. Then we'll go to your accident scene."

The door opened behind the paramedics. Two hospital security guards stepped out.

"There a problem here?" one of the guards asked.

"Fellow here wants to report an accident by stealing an

ambulance. Dropped Kershaw's name as the reason."

Aaron had heard enough. He hopped inside the ambulance, slammed the door, and dropped the locks. When he reached for the keys, the guards outside yelled at him to stop at the same time, the radio blasted.

Aaron let his hand fall from the keys. The second paramedic was still inside the passenger side of the vehicle, holding the radio.

The call came in about a fire at the psychiatric hospital, and ambulances were needed.

Aaron's stomach dropped at those words. *Sarah* ...

"What hospital?" the attendant asked into the radio.

"The Amy Greg Psychiatric Hospital," Aaron said, urgency in his voice. "That's what I've been trying to tell you."

A second later, the radio crackled, "The Amy Greg Psychiatric Hospital."

The attendant met his eyes. "Unlock the door and let the driver in. Then get back there." He pointed into the back as he held the mic to his mouth and told the dispatcher they were attending the fire.

Moments later, as the trio drove from the hospital property, Aaron leaned forward and said, "Drive faster. And use the fucking sirens."

He stared through the windshield the entire way, Sarah's name running through his head.

"I'm coming, baby."

Chapter 22

SARAH HAD MANAGED TO turn the bed in such a way as to get herself facing the door. When she flipped the bed onto its side, she could get down on her hands and knees and suck clean air in from the corridor from under the door.

She hacked and coughed, remembering a church in Los Angeles where she hid in the crypt until the fire was extinguished.

More like passed out in the crypt.

Feet shuffled by the door. Maybe someone would spot the key and push it back to her or, better yet, open the door.

"Hey—" her voice caught in her throat. She swallowed, cleared her mouth, and tried again. "Help!"

The shuffling stopped.

"The key. To my room. It's on the floor." She swallowed hard, then coughed. "Please. There's a fire in here. The key."

She jumped at the shrill sound of the fire alarm, jerking

her left wrist. She winced with the pain.

Shit, how the hell do I get myself into these messes?

"Help," she shouted, but the alarm drowned out her voice. "The key," she tried again before the coughing started. She hacked over and over as smoke began to escape through the recesses of the door, cutting off any chance of clean air.

A metallic sound chunked above her. Someone had inserted a key.

She rolled out of the way, but not far enough. The door opened and smacked into the small of her back.

"Dammit!" she shouted, but the fire alarm drowned her voice out again. She could barely hear herself; the alarm was so loud.

Two hospital staff rushed in.

"Move out of the way," the one holding a fire extinguisher yelled.

The other wore a long white coat with a crazy thick mustache. He tried to right the bed she was still attached to, but it got stuck on her wrists, twisting her arms at odd angles.

She grunted in protest, held them up to show him, and then coughed again. The fire was almost out, smoke filling the room. The attendant was using the extinguisher on Dr. Williams now. She hadn't noticed when she was on the floor breathing through the opening at the base of the door, but the fire had started to burn through Williams's clothes. Whether dead or unconscious, he hadn't responded to the flames licking his body.

That was a bad sign for her, but she didn't care. She needed to focus on Cole now. Taking it all in, she knew they would blame everything on her. She killed the doctor. She set the fire. Sarah would be detained, which is what Cole needed so he could get away. Sarah would be held responsible for this arson without evidence untouched by flames in those boxes to implicate Cole and cast suspicion elsewhere.

There was no easy way to look at it.

Not only that, the authorities were looking for her about a dead woman found in her car, unless Williams was lying.

The only way out of this was to leave, locate Cole and finish it. He'd confess to whatever she wanted him to when she was done with him.

The fire was out now, only smoke clouded the air, but that was dissipating quickly. The bed was back on its wheels, and both attendants were looking at her hands as they rested on the front corners, still tied as they were.

The alarm silenced, leaving behind a ringing in her ears.

"I bet you two are wondering what happened here?" she said.

They looked at each other in slow motion. Then, just as slowly, they turned back to her. Without looking into it or asking her side of things, they had decided exactly what had happened here. The doctor was on the floor. The patient was trying to escape. The patient, a pyromaniac as she had the Macdonald Triad of psychosis, had set the fire.

They had one job: contain the patient.

"Well, at least let me explain myself," Sarah said, her fingers tightening around the edge of the bed. "As I was about to be raped and then burned to death, I chose to fight back." She shrugged. "Believe me?"

The man with the fire extinguisher took a step forward. Mustache Man reached into the pocket of his white coat for something.

"I didn't think so," she said, "Anyway, gotta go."

She shoved the bed forward, spinning it sideways to hit the attendant with the extinguisher and clothesline Mustache Man. The clothesline worked, knocking the attendant, his hand still in his pocket, onto his ass. But the fire extinguisher attendant dodged. Before Sarah could straighten it out and exit the room backward through the wide open door, he grabbed the end and held firm.

With a strong yank, she almost snapped it out of his grasp. Mustache Man was already getting up off the floor.

Forcefully, performing a version of bed tug of war, she backed out of the room as the attendant holding the other end of the bed slipped on the leftover foam from the fire extinguisher. People walked back and forth behind her in the corridor. Rooms were open, patients stumbling around, some agitated, their mental state disrupted with the violence of the alarm moments before.

Two feet out the door, someone banged into her back as they scuttled by. A woman shrieked from Sarah's left side. An old man with graying hair stopped and peeked into her room. He looked back at Sarah with a blank stare on his face.

Then Mustache Man, a syringe in hand, jumped up on the bed, a wicked grin on his face. The bed blocked the entrance to the room as the other attendant held firm to his side. She had nowhere to go and, tied to the bed as she was, would not be able to escape the needle.

In quiet desperation, she gritted her teeth, clenched her jaw, leaned back, and planted her feet, pulling and yanking, but it was useless. With the other guy pulling back and the mustache man on the bed, she was stuck.

He crawled forward and hopped off on her side.

"You're really something, aren't you?" he said, waving

the needle back and forth. "Thought you could kill your doctor and just walk out of here?"

"Something like that. Truth is elusive. Like me. Elusive." She winked.

"Somehow, I doubt that, crazy bitch." He stepped toward her.

"Buck Cherry."

He stopped and looked at his partner, who had climbed up on the bed and was exiting the room on the bed that still blocked the door.

"What?"

"You just quoted a song by them. Buck Cherry sings a song called Crazy Bitch."

"Fuckin' looney tunes is what you are." He took the last step toward her. "Hold her," he said to the other guy.

The patients sauntering about had thickened. Some scrabbled on the floor by the wall as if they were searching for lost coins or mementos of a past when sanity wasn't so fleeting.

Sarah stepped back from them but didn't have far to go as someone moved in between the mustache man and her.

Helena, the woman who stuck her head in Sarah's door earlier and told her about the burning that comes in the night.

"No one touches her," Helena shouted.

The other attendant shoved Helena aside, then turned to Sarah, his nostrils flaring, eyes red.

"You'll go down heavy for this, and I'll be there to watch you suffer in here where you'll rot away under my loving care."

"Fuck you. I'll kill you next."

Then Helena was back. She landed on the attendant's

back, wailing and shrieking, pulling clumps of his hair out. The patients around them stirred into a frenzy. The look of fright on the mustache man's face intensified as he fought off two old men who crowded him.

Sarah eased the bed back and stepped away from the pandemonium as it grew in degrees by the second. One moment they were talking in the corridor, the next, five patients were taking down Mustache Man as Helena still clung to the other attendant, who was now on his knees.

"Should've treated them better," Sarah shouted. "Consequences are always due, paid in full."

When she had an available room, she swung the bed around and started down the hallway, her wrists chafed and raw now from all the twisting and turning.

At the end of the hall, the door leading to the dining room was wide open. She pushed through it and continued to parts unknown.

Then another alarm sounded.

People from the acute ward were escaping. Court-ordered patients were getting out. A full-scale riot was taking place in front of her old room. Backup was coming. The odds of leaving decreased every second she was still inside, cuffed to a bed on wheels.

"Vivian! What now?" she asked as she hit a door on the other side of the dining room.

It was locked.

When she turned around, three men in white coats, two flanking the one with a needle held high, entered on the other side. The two on either side had to be the muscle, with one at least six and a half feet tall.

"Got something here to put you to sleep." The man held

the needle high with pride like an Olympic torch. "For a century."

Sarah pushed down on her side of the bed, lifted the other end, and spun it around to face the trio.

"I was told three assholes would show up for dinner. I didn't believe them. Man, was I wrong." She lowered her head, closed her eyes, and whispered to Vivian. Images of Vivian's violation filtered through, bringing goosebumps to her arms and neck. Fury seethed through her. She inhaled deeply, tightened her jaw, and looked up.

All three men started running at her.

Chapter 23

Firefighters were already on the scene. Police cruisers were coming in behind the ambulance as Aaron's driver pulled up to the front doors.

"Try to stay out of the way," the driver said as he exited the vehicle.

Aaron jumped out and stayed off to the side. When he was sure no one was watching him, he started for the side of the building. Firemen ran in the front doors, followed by paramedics. Police stood around and talked to nurses and male attendants. It was chaos but under control. That allowed him to become unseen.

He used bushes for cover as he slipped along the side of the building until he reached an open door. Adults in disarray, some dressed in pajamas, some in robes, loitered in the area of the trimmed hedges. Some stood on the finely cut grass, and others wandered back and forth along the sidewalk. One old woman mumbled to herself, and another argued with a wooden bench. A man wore something on his head that resembled a hockey helmet. He felt sorry for the lot of them and the mental demons they carried.

Then he turned, entered through the open side door, and ran along a corridor, knocking doors open and shouting Sarah's name.

If she were in here somewhere, he would find her.

If someone had hurt her, he would hurt them.

If someone had killed her—

He let the thought go as he unlocked the door at the end of the hall and entered a dining area littered with tables and chairs.

To his surprise, Sarah was right in front of him. From five feet away, he saw that she was tied to a gurney or bed on wheels of some kind. She appeared to be using it as a weapon between her and the three men who were advancing from across the wide room.

"Hey!" Aaron shouted. Sarah spun toward his voice, her hair flying up. He broke into a run, heading straight for the largest man, who had to be over six feet tall.

The man slowed and prepared for Aaron, but nothing could be ready for Aaron's anger, his raw fury at seeing Sarah in this state.

Three quick strides later, and he was on them. A fast jump to give them the wrong impression, and then Aaron slipped to the floor, slid a few feet on the polished wood, and jabbed open-palmed at the large man's heels before he could retreat. Aaron counted on the large man being slow on his feet. The contact was clean, snapping something on the inside. The six-foot-plus man yelped and dropped hard, the floor vibrating with the fall. Aaron rolled twice to avoid being landed on.

Aaron rose to his feet and ran at the remaining two. The man in the middle held a syringe and continued toward Sarah, but the other had turned to challenge Aaron.

He stepped in close to the guy, who grabbed Aaron's lapels in both hands. Aaron shot his right arm across his body to dislodge one of the man's hands from his shirt, then lifted his arm up high, spun it out, and around the man's other arm that still held on. After it was fully wrapped, Aaron lifted up, trapping the man's arm. His opponent's elbow bent in a way it wasn't made to. When the pressure was at the breaking point, Aaron jerked upward. The man's elbow popped under the strain. He screeched when Aaron released the arm, and it flopped the opposite way, bouncing in a sick fashion. The man fell to his knees, staring at his ruined arm as if it was a mad disease about to consume him.

Aaron wasted no time admiring his handiwork as he turned his attention to the last man, still holding the needle, who had stopped to watch what Aaron had done.

"You aren't a patient," the man said, more a statement than a question.

"Drop the needle and walk away, or you'll be a patient at the local hospital for a long time." He pointed at Sarah and bellowed, deep and raspy, "Nobody threatens my woman."

People were entering the cavernous room behind Aaron. He heard them but didn't turn around.

"Aaron." Parkman's voice, warning, cautioning. "The police are here now. That's enough."

"It's never enough. Drop the fucking needle and step off."

The man seemed to think about it. Aaron stepped forward and jerked as if he was going to jab or punch. The man flinched and tossed the needle. It landed harmlessly ten feet away.

"There," the man said. "You happy?"

Aaron moved toward Sarah. As he stepped past the man, he elbowed the side of his head. The guy yelped and bent at the waist.

"Now I'm happy," Aaron said as he wrapped his arms around Sarah. She couldn't hug him back as her hands were still bed-bound. "Are you okay?"

She nodded against his shoulder.

People stepped in closer, uniformed police officers surrounding them.

"Sarah Roberts," Kershaw said. "You're going to have to come with us."

She pulled back from Aaron. "Am I under arrest?" she asked.

"We'll talk at the station."

"I'm not going anywhere with you." Sarah turned to Aaron. "Find me some keys and get me the hell out of these things. Then take me to a hotel. I need sleep, food, and whiskey, but not in that order."

"I'm afraid I can't let you do that," Kershaw said.

"Why the fuck not?" Aaron asked, moving toward Kershaw.

Parkman's hand landed on Aaron's shoulder. "Calm, man. This is Kershaw. He isn't the enemy. Be cool."

"A woman," Kershaw said, "as of yet to be identified, was found deceased in Sarah's car. There are other questions that need answering, like what happened here. Once everything is sorted out, we'll see where that takes us. But for now, I'm requesting Sarah come with us." He faced Sarah, a stern grimace creasing his features. "If you refuse, I will have to arrest you."

Sarah redirected her attention to Aaron's eyes. "It's okay. I'll go with him."

"You know how I feel about this," Aaron said, directing it to Kershaw.

"I know what I'm doing," Sarah said to him.

Aaron stepped back.

Sarah addressed Kershaw, the bed shaking. "I go willingly on one condition."

Kershaw raised his eyebrows and glanced at Parkman, who smiled and nodded. "What's the condition?" Kershaw asked.

"Through that door and down the hall." She pointed. "Inside the room that had the fire, there's a pile of boxes. Some of them burned, and some weren't. Inside those boxes, you'll find a lot of interesting documents. Proof and evidence that was meant to be destroyed in the fire. Retrieve that, seize it, tell them you're taking it out to be destroyed, get a warrant, whatever. I don't care how you do it, just get them and keep them safe. Then I'll come willingly. Those are my terms. Meet those terms, or a lot of people will be visiting the hospital because I've got a very angry pit bull beside me who will do as I say."

"Fuckin' right," Aaron shouted. "Who's first?"

Kershaw moved closer to Sarah. "I won't agree to those terms because you're coming with us whether you want to or not. My officers won't be cowed or threatened. But I will secure those items because it's something I want to do." He motioned for his men to leave. Three men ran out of the dining area toward the room that had burned. "Because of my long-term friendship with Parkman, and I know how he feels about you, I'll let your threat go." He stepped back and spoke to the officers behind her. "Undo those cuffs and take her to the car." He stole a glance at Aaron. "Take him, too."

"Fuck this up, Kershaw, and it'll be your career," Sarah said. "I'll see to it. That's not a threat. That's a promise, and I never bluff. If you lose Cole Lincoln, he will strike again. Take me for now. But it's Cole you should be after."

"Tell me all that and more at the station."

Two men grabbed Aaron's arms and led him away. He allowed it as struggle now would be futile. As he neared the door, he heard Kershaw ask Sarah a question.

"Tell me, Sarah, how did you know my name?" Kershaw asked. "We haven't met."

"Sometimes, I just know things," Sarah said.

Aaron looked over his shoulder. She was turned toward Parkman as they worked on her wrist cuffs. "Or maybe Parkman used it once already. Come on, Kershaw. Is that the extent of your detective career? You're going to have to be more observant."

"Get her out of here," Kershaw shouted.

They led Sarah away, a large smile on her face.

Aaron turned around and was led away.

Chapter 24

THE CELL WAS SMALL and uncomfortable, but it allowed her to rest. As a holding cell, it was better than a dank prison cell. Early morning light spilled across the bed. A toilet sat behind a partition, and there was a sink she could drink from. The food wasn't great, but Kershaw had delivered it himself. He was trying to make peace with her, which had more to do with Parkman and their friendship than with her.

Kershaw had provided clothes before she fell asleep last night. The pants had a stretchy elastic waist, so they fit snuggly, but the shirt's sleeves were too long, so she had to roll them up. It wasn't a bother, though. There were more important things in life to worry about than if the clothes fit properly.

Staring at the ceiling, she tried to piece together what role Vivian had played recently. Overall, Sarah had been tossed around a bit but was relatively unhurt. Whatever evidence in those boxes that were meant to burn had been recovered. Kershaw told her when he brought the clothes that his men were going through them one by one.

Whatever was discovered in those boxes had to implicate Dr. Williams—who died in the fire—and Cole Lincoln in several of the crimes they were involved in. Otherwise, why did they try to burn the boxes? Last she heard, no one knew where Cole had gone. He had disappeared at the end of his shift. By now, the morning after, he could be anywhere.

With all that going on—Sarah locked up in a cell and Aaron in another one—where was Vivian? What was Parkman up to?

Most importantly, was her role in this over?

The memories that had haunted Sarah had diminished. Were those memories planted to entice Sarah into therapy? If so, that meant Vivian could control everything that Sarah was exposed to, even her brain waves and thoughts.

"Why not?" Sarah said out loud. "You've controlled me physically before. All this time, it's been your show. I'm just the willing puppet."

She curled up in a ball and tried to figure her life out. Maybe it was time to relax a little and stay calm. Just chill. Go back to answering random messages from Vivian. Ones that included a fistfight or a purse snatching. Something easy.

Before she was shot in the head in Toronto a while back, she had expressed her feelings to Aaron—how she wanted to quit the dangerous vigilante life for good and begin a normal family, a regular existence. But a bullet to the skull had changed that and made her realize just how much she was needed. She had been ungrateful of the gift, the ability to talk to someone from the other side who had foreknowledge of ominous things to come. Someone who could save her life when needed, step in and take over even when Sarah was powerless or drugged. Sarah trusted Vivian implicitly, and that hadn't wavered. If those rape images were planted in her mind to elicit a specific response, it worked. If Vivian led Sarah to Cole, Sarah had to be the willing puppet. In the end, it justified the means.

She had learned to trust the process years ago, but that didn't stop her from questioning it occasionally. And there was a quiet assurance that Vivian wouldn't ever give her something she truly couldn't handle.

A lock clicked down the hall. Footsteps approached.

"Sarah Roberts?" a man asked.

She got up off the bed and approached the bars.

A uniformed officer came into view. He reminded her of a young David Caruso when the actor played a cop in the original Rambo movie.

"Kershaw wants to speak with you."

"Really? Tell him to leave a message. I've got appointments all day."

She walked back to the bed and stretched out on it.

"Very funny." He slid the door aside. "Get up. Let's go. Kershaw has good news. You're going to want to hear it. Follow me."

She rolled over and eyed him. "I guess it couldn't hurt to hear what he has to say."

Sarah followed him up the corridor toward the front offices.

"What was the name of the first Rambo movie?" she asked.

"*First Blood*," the officer said over his shoulder.

"Right, thanks."

At the door, he stopped. "Why did you ask about *First Blood*?"

"You remind me of Caruso in that movie."

The young cop shook his head, a sheepish grin on his face. "Everyone says that. Shit, I hate it."

"Why? Caruso's a great actor."

"I just want to be known for me, for who I am."

"Doesn't everybody." She walked through the door and made a beeline for Kershaw's office, the escort officer staying close. Sarah wondered how *I just want to be known for who I am* related to her. She was known for who she was, even though Vivian was responsible for most of her actions.

How lucky am I?

At the glass door to Kershaw's office, she knocked. Kershaw looked up and waved her in.

"You can go, Officer Douglas," Kershaw said.

The door closed behind her.

"Take a seat, Sarah." He gestured at one of the chairs opposite his desk.

Sarah decided on the chair out of the sun beaming through the window. The office was full of trophies, plaques, family pictures, and sports memorabilia.

"You a baseball fan or a football fan?" she asked.

"Both."

On his desk sat a large golf trophy.

"Golf, too?"

He nodded. "But we aren't sitting across from each other to discuss sports. With all the scumbags I deal with daily, I need my office to have as much of me as it can have to maintain some semblance of sanity."

"Makes sense."

"Got a call this morning."

"From?"

"A woman claiming to be the sister of the dead woman found in your car yesterday." He paused to lean back in his chair. It creaked under the strain. He tented his fingers and stared at her.

"And?" Sarah prompted.

"It *was* her sister."

"Great."

Sarah waited. It looked like Kershaw would spill whatever he knew over the next ten hours unless she was willing to draw it out of him, sentence by sentence. But this tête à tête was his show. So she leaned back in her chair, crossed her legs, and waited, her face expressionless.

"Just like in the movies, this sister received a letter. One of those in-the-unfortunate-event-that-I-die letters. It spilled the beans on Cole Lincoln." Kershaw waggled his eyebrows up and down, then stopped when Sarah stayed expressionless. "The sister, the dead woman, feared Cole would have her killed. Her last debt repayment was to play the role of a receptionist for a legitimate psychologist named Dr. Lance Williams. According to the letter, the job seemed legit, so she agreed to it. I'm assuming that was to lure you to him."

"Does the letter mention why she had the debt to Cole?"

Kershaw shook his head.

"Sounds like you've solved the murder in my car. So I'm free to go?"

Kershaw got up from his chair and turned to stare out the window. "You don't seem overly excited that we have a letter, something that sways your attention from you."

"I didn't kill the woman. I know that. I was the victim here. I'm lucky you aren't wiping my burnt skin off the floor of that room today and using my teeth to identify me. I was locked inside a psych *acute* ward with no hope of getting out alive, so no, I'm not terribly excited about anything right now. I'm ready to move on. Now that you have all that you need on Cole Lincoln, I can leave it well enough alone."

Kershaw turned to her. "Parkman and I go way back. He told me a little about you. There's no way you'll *move on*, as you put it."

She shrugged. "Why stay involved? With your resources, you could have Cole picked up by tonight and the charges filed for his arraignment in the morning. What else is there for me? He'll be up on murder one and then some. Sounds premeditated to me." She stood and brushed her hands back and forth, slapping them together as if to clear unwanted dirt. "We're good here. I'm done."

Kershaw walked around his desk and stopped in front of her.

"Why don't I believe you?" he asked.

"Because you don't know me. Now, whether you believe me or not, am I free to go?"

Kershaw nodded. "But stick around. I may want to talk to you again."

"I'll be at my cabin. I'm sure you know where that is."

"It's a mess up there."

"So I've heard. But for now, that's where I'll be. And Aaron? Is he free to go?"

"Already gone with Parkman last night."

She reached the door and turned back. "I thought you

detained him?"

"I did. For all of half an hour. Just to calm him down. That guy can be dangerous."

"Agreed. Oh, my car keys?"

Kershaw shook his head. "Can't do that. You're carless."

"And why's that?"

"Forensics still has your Charger in the shop. There was a murder committed in it, after all. Gotta work all the angles."

"When they're done with it, have it brought to me at the cabin."

"Yes, ma'am!" Kershaw said, his voice raised an octave.

Sarah slammed the door on her way out.

Chapter 25

Sarah instructed the cab driver to stop and let her out half a mile from the cabin. As the cab pulled away from the shoulder of the road, she headed in the opposite direction of the cabin. In the warmth of the spring day, she hiked up her sleeves.

A full minute later, the taxi was out of sight. A ninety-degree turn to the right brought her over the shoulder of the road, down the embankment, and into the cover of trees. With Cole and those two men who drugged her in Williams's office still out there, she wanted to reconnoiter the area before walking into the cabin unarmed, straight into an ambush.

Stepping over the fallen branches and dead leaves that littered the floor of the woods surrounding her cabin, she tried to remember the last place she had put her gun. It was probably still stowed behind the night table by the bed unless the men who ransacked the cabin found it.

Mindful of noise, she watched every step, placing her feet gently, and only paused when the sound of a vehicle traveling by on the road. When her cabin came into view, nothing seemed out of place. No vehicle was in the driveway, and the front door was closed but sitting askew. To an outsider, it would appear that no one was home and everything was fine.

She leaned back against a tree and waited, watching the cabin and the driveway while she listened to the traffic on the main road. After about ten minutes, she asked Vivian if she needed to know anything.

Vivian was silent.

Which meant nothing. Only that Sarah probably wasn't about to die. Although she wouldn't put it past Vivian to forget to mention that little detail.

She pushed off the tree and walked fifty yards to the cabin. Once there, she walked around it, front to back, looking in the windows, testing to see if they were locked.

Even though Vivian was quiet, not even the slightest feeling of her presence, Sarah felt something was off. She couldn't explain it. It was like there was tension in the air.

At the front door, she spun the knob and shoved the door hard enough for it to smack into the inside wall. A quick peek inside revealed nothing untoward except the ransacked mess. No one had cleaned up a thing since it was ripped apart. Whoever came through was bent on destruction. The furniture was flipped over, broken, and sliced apart, stuffing protruding from the couch's cushions. The little kitchen area was covered in broken dishes and glasses. The table where she had her computer was broken into four pieces, one piece sitting in the doorway to the bedroom.

"What the hell?" she whispered to herself, shaking her head.

Anger stirred inside. Why do this? Just to get her? To make her pay for the repairs to the rental unit? Too petty. To anger her? Too immature. Maybe they were sending a message. Leave a dead body in her car. Ransack her cabin. Commit her for being insane, and then she dies in the fire she supposedly set. A lot of people might buy that story, but Parkman and Aaron wouldn't have.

She walked over broken table pieces and recliner chair stuffing toward the bedroom. Inside the room, nothing was any different than the rest of the cabin. The bed frame was destroyed, and the mattress was gutted. But the night tables on either side were intact. She rushed over to the one on her side of the bed, pulled it away from the wall, and slapped her hand on the back.

The Glock was gone.

"Looking for this?" a man said.

Sarah snapped around, hands up in a defensive posture. After a brief moment, she lowered her hands and stood up straight.

One of the men from the cemetery leaned on the doorframe, her gun hung loosely from his hand in a non-threatening way. The implied threat was evident: move, and the gun would be brought to bear. Attack, and the gun would fire.

"How?" Sarah asked.

"Luck. I saw you coming and stayed on the opposite side of the house. At one point, I thought you saw me, but—"

Sarah shook her head. "That's not what I wanted to

know."

He frowned and pushed off from the door. "Then how what?"

"How are you such an asshole?"

His lips tightened as if he was going to snarl. It reminded her of a dog, which made her smile.

He started across the room toward her. "Why are you smiling?"

"Because of my sister."

"Huh?"

He stopped in front of her.

"Yeah, my sister. She didn't mention I'd see you here. Crazy, huh?"

"Yeah, crazy. Maybe that's why Williams wanted you in that hospital for dummies."

"It's not a hospital for dummies—" she cut herself off, gasped, and ducked as if a threat was at the bedroom window.

The man jerked out of reflex and looked at the window. Already low, the center of gravity balanced, Sarah drove her fist into his groin using her hips for momentum. Upon contact, the gun became her focus.

It all happened in a second. He was spinning back to her when her fist made contact. Then his gun hand was wrenched back, and the Glock forcefully ripped from his grasp. He shrieked at the pain between his legs and gave little resistance, or thought, to the gun, which was a mistake.

She spun it around, slipped her finger inside the trigger guard, and almost pulled the trigger.

"Step off. Move back."

"Fuck you," he said, his voice an octave higher than

moments ago.

"As you wish."

She pulled the trigger. It clicked empty.

"You stupid bitch," he groaned through clenched teeth. "You think I'd get this close to you with a loaded weapon?"

With both hands wrapped around the butt of the gun and too close to him, she barely blocked the backhanded fist that came for her face. All she succeeded in doing was bumping his forearm.

Stars swam in her vision. She refocused, tossed the gun aside, and went on the offensive, both hands flailing in fisted jabs. Only the first two landed before he was out of reach.

"Enough of this stupidity," another, deeper voice said. "We haven't got time to play high school fighting games. Grab her, and let's go."

Sarah turned toward the speaker. It was the other man from the cemetery.

His partner leaned against the bedroom wall, holding his crotch.

"Stop being a baby. I brought the car around. It's parked out front. Bring her, and let's go."

"She's a handful," he said.

Sarah lowered her fists. The stars had disappeared, but a dull throbbing began where he'd hit her.

The man at the door also had a weapon. This one was probably loaded.

"There's no play here, woman," he said. "You see that, don't you?"

Sarah nodded. "No play." Weaponless and up against the bedroom wall, there really was nothing she could do. If he wanted her dead, he could just shoot her. But the Glock had been empty on purpose. The only reason was that their employer probably wanted her alive. He wanted her alive and well because Cole Lincoln wouldn't want it any other way.

"On second thought, I do have a play."

The man at the door steadied his weapon, the barrel now aimed at her.

"And what play is that?" he asked.

"To come with you."

He lowered his weapon. "That's not a play."

"It is if I choose to do it willingly."

"I've got the gun. It isn't willingly."

"I assure you, it is."

She stepped over the junk on the floor and walked past the man, still holding his crotch.

"This girl is psycho, man. When the boss is done with her, I want her head."

She looked back over her shoulder. "My head? How odd? I would think you'd want another body part."

"No, stupid bitch, just your head. So I can crush it with a hammer."

"Ohhh, how inventive." She acted like she had chills all over as she held her arms together across her chest and shook as if afraid. "So scary. Bash my head in." She dropped her arms and stared at the man in the doorway. In a deep voice, she said, "Take me to your leader."

"Fuck off," he shouted and backhanded her with his gun hand before she could stop him or block it.

Her head snapped sideways, but she stayed on her feet. When she righted herself, the copper taste of blood filled her mouth and spilled over her lips. A couple of teeth felt loose but were too numbed from the blow to be sure.

"That was for what you did to Frank. Now start walking for the car like a good little girl."

She smiled wide, sure her white teeth would be crimson with blood.

"I will kill you for that."

"I'm sure you will, Princess." He shoved her shoulder and brought the gun up again. "Move toward the car or take another shot to the head. The next one will be lights out."

Sarah wiped her lips and cleaned her hand on her pants. Then she spit a gob of blood on the dirty floor at her feet. "The enzymes that digest your food start to eat you on the inside approximately three days after death." She met his eyes. "You ready for that? Not just rotting, but being eaten from the inside as well?"

He just stared at her. Possibly trying to comprehend what he was looking at. Most girls wouldn't respond to a crushing blow to the mouth like Sarah did.

But that was what made her who she was.

Cole Lincoln had no idea who was coming for him. He wouldn't have sent two men to pick her up if he did.

That was like a snitch or mafia informer sending two men to grab the hitman contracted out to kill him, thereby delivering the hitman to his hit.

Stupid, stupid move.

But most who chose the life of crime were stupid. Violent, but stupid. If a blow to the face was all it took to be escorted to Cole's door, she would take two, please.

She started for the cabin's door.

"Coming?" she asked over her shoulder as she stepped out into the sun.

They followed her to their car.

"Stop," the man who had hit her with the gun shouted from behind her.

Sarah stopped near the rear of the vehicle.

He walked around her to the trunk, opened it, and pulled out a pair of jeans and a black T-shirt.

"Take off your clothes," he said.

"Fuck you."

He snickered and stepped closer, holding the clothes out to her.

"We don't have time to play. Now, change into these so we can get out of here."

"How do you know my size?"

"If these don't fit, I've got two more pairs, just in case. Wouldn't want you to have to be naked."

When she didn't move toward the clothes he offered, he raised his gun.

"Come on. Don't be stupid. Just strip and put these on. I promise I won't look."

She grabbed the clothes and looked around for Frank, but he was nowhere to be seen. The bushes at the back of the car looked inviting. She nodded toward them, but he shook his head.

"Right here. You're not leaving my sight."

She waited another moment, holding the clothes, trying to decide if she would protest again or not.

"My instructions are to deliver you alive. He didn't say anything about being injured or close to death. Hurry and change, or I will shoot you in the foot and watch you bleed for the next few hours we're together."

She watched his face. His eyes saw the look there and believed him. Turning slightly away, she slipped out of the pants Kershaw gave her and put the jeans on. They were one size too big but fit well enough. Then the shirt. Once she was dressed, she handed him her old clothes.

"Now get in the car."

In the back seat, she looked out at the cabin where Frank had resurfaced. He walked without a limp. The pain in his crotch must've worn off. He held a red gas can.

What is it with these guys and fire?

Frank and his gun-toting partner, who held the clothes Kershaw had given her, stepped back, closer to the car. Then Frank threw something, and a ball of flame shot up, obscuring the front of the cabin in orange. As suddenly as it had ignited, it died down, but a part of the fire remained, licking up the wooden walls.

Maybe it was better this way. The people she rented it from could collect the insurance and rebuild. Trying to fix what was broken wasn't as appealing as just rebuilding.

Frank headed for the passenger side while his partner waited a moment longer. Then he tossed Sarah's clothes on the perimeter of the fire and got in the driver's seat.

"As far as the world is concerned, Sarah Roberts is dead." He twisted in the seat to look back at her. "When they come here and see your clothes burnt, they'll assume the worst. Once a fire marshal concludes his investigation and they have not discovered a body, a search will start, but it'll be too late. Far too late."

"There are more important things for me to worry about," she said.

"Like what?" he asked.

"My gun. I want it back when this is all done. I love that thing."

"You're a strange one."

"If you only knew."

"I'm learning." He produced what looked like a dart gun. "Sleep a while, strange girl."

Before she could smack it from his hand, a small dart with a red feather on the end entered her thigh.

Her hand slipped off the end of the dart when she tried to pull it from her skin. On the second try, she slipped sideways in the seat, her cheek bumping the car window, all her strength used up.

"Strange girl?" she said. "No. Stranger danger. Thass me …"

She thought she heard him say something else as she went under, but she only caught the word bitch.

Before the lights went out, she whispered one more word.

Vivian ...

Chapter 26

"WHERE SHOULD WE START?" Aaron asked as Parkman pulled out of the drive-thru with two fresh coffees.

They had arrived at the police station to discover Sarah had been released. Kershaw said he had no cause to hold her any longer and had been too busy to call either Parkman or Aaron yet, the latter of which became animatedly angry.

Parkman pulled Aaron out of the police station, calmed him down, and drove for coffee.

"She's probably back at the cabin," Parkman said. He had no idea where else to look for Sarah, and she wouldn't have gone too far without a car. He looked at Aaron sideways. "Head there?"

Aaron nodded. "Sure. Head to the cabin. Maybe she's there cleaning it up."

Parkman drove down the main street and sped up as he exited town. Movement in the mirror caught his eye. He set his coffee down in the cup holder.

"Where's that siren coming from?" Aaron asked.

"Fire trucks and an ambulance racing up behind us." Parkman slowed and eased off the road to let them pass.

Aaron spun in his seat to look out the back window. "You don't think?" he asked, leaving the sentence hanging.

"There's one way to find out."

He grabbed his cell and dialed Kershaw. As it rang on Kershaw's end, the firetrucks passed Parkman's car. Then the ambulance followed. He checked his mirrors, saw the road was clear, then pulled back onto the road.

When the phone picked up, Parkman had to pull it away from his ear.

"Kershaw?"

"Yeah. Parkman?"

"What's going on? Where are you?"

"Heading out to a fire."

"Firetrucks just passed us. Where are they headed?"

"Call came in when you guys left for coffee."

"And?"

"It's Sarah's cabin. I'm sorry, Parkman."

"Sarah's cabin?"

"Yeah—"

Parkman dropped the phone and slammed the gas pedal down.

Fifteen minutes later, half a mile from the cabin, he could already see the flames. Emergency lights rotated on the tops of the vehicles surrounding the front entrance to the cabin. He parked as close as he could and hopped out with Aaron on his heels. Parkman's stomach twisted at the likelihood that Sarah was still inside.

For the duration of the drive to the cabin, Aaron sat quietly beside him, staring out the window. At one point, Parkman caught Aaron crying.

Now Aaron stood beside him, looking at what was once a beautiful cabin, the now burned-out shell of a building.

A police car screeched to a halt behind them, and Kershaw jumped out. He ran over.

"Parkman," he said, trying to catch his breath. "Learn anything?"

"Just got here." His voice sounded distant to himself, monotone.

They watched as firemen attacked the flames. Kershaw stepped forward, staring at the ground beside the gravel driveway. He waited as a fireman worked a hose nearby, then when he had a break, Kershaw sprang forward and picked something up off the ground. He turned back to Parkman and Aaron and headed their way.

"What's that?" Aaron asked.

"Can you control him?" Kershaw said, staring at Parkman, who nodded.

"Aaron's not stupid. He'll be cool, or he'll chill in a cell. He knows that. Now, whose clothes are those? Stretchy pants aren't something Sarah would wear, and they're slightly burnt. Do you recognize them?"

Kershaw nodded. "Oh, I recognize them all right."

"How?" Aaron asked, stepping closer.

"When Sarah left the Amy Greg Facility, I was able to rustle up some clothes for her." Kershaw held the pants and shirt with long sleeves up in the air. "These were those clothes."

"Which means what, exactly?" Parkman asked.

"She's either naked out there somewhere—" he pointed past Parkman and Aaron. "Or she's in there and didn't need these anymore. People rarely commit suicide by arson, so I suspect someone was waiting for her here."

"Arson?" Parkman asked.

"Those gas cans tipped me off." Kershaw pointed.

Parkman's eyes followed Kershaw's finger. Three red gas cans were piled against one another in the grass by the base of a tree.

"And you just let her go?" Aaron shouted. "With Cole still out there?"

Parkman wrapped an arm around Aaron and eased him back a few steps.

"C'mon, Aaron. There's nothing we can do here."

"You know what, Parkman, I'm done *doing*. It's always you and me trying to find Sarah. After she was shot in the head, we went across the country looking for her. Then in Canada, we chased her. If it wasn't for you, that cannibal would've eaten her." He met Parkman's eyes, then turned from him. "Forget about it. I'm done."

Aaron walked away, headed for the car. After a deep breath, Parkman followed him. Once in the car, Parkman put a hand on Aaron's shoulder.

"What's going on?" he asked.

Aaron fiddled with his fingers as he watched the fire. "I'm just tired of it all. I signed on for Sarah. Not this."

"Me too, Aaron, me too."

"No, I mean tired, as in, not sure I want to continue doing this."

"How so?" Parkman asked.

"I haven't been comfortable with Sarah's choice for a

long time. I mean, I love what she does for other people, but the risks she takes are too great. I know she gives great speeches about being duty-bound and shit, but just when we're finally getting to spend lots of time together training, reading, watching movies, and really enjoying ourselves, something happens, and off she goes to save someone else. Then here we are, picking up the pieces, trying to find her. I don't know if she's being raped, tortured, or already dead. I love her, Parkman, but I can't keep doing this. I've got a dojo to run. I'm supposed to be heading back to Toronto."

"I know, I know." He patted Aaron's shoulder.

"No, you don't. Because you've been with her since the Armond Stuart days, and you're still here, picking up the pieces."

"Because I don't just believe in Sarah. I believe in Vivian."

"Meaning what?"

"That Sarah will be okay in the end. She always is. Sure, scrapes, bruises, sometimes broken bones, and even bullet holes, but overall, Sarah's a fighter and a lifer. She'll do this job until she physically can't. That's the only thing that'll stop her."

"Okay, fair enough, but I can't keep doing it."

"What are you saying? You're walking away, leaving Sarah? What'll you do? Head back to Toronto?"

"No, I'll try to stick around until we find her. If she's alive, I'll talk to her about this. I'll tell her how I feel. But then, I'm gone. When she quits this job one day, I'll be there for her."

Parkman stared out the front window. He wondered how Sarah would take Aaron's departure. "Prepare yourself for a long wait. She's never going to quit. Only death will stop her, and even then, with Sarah, you can never be too sure."

Aaron wiped at his eyes. "I just love her too much to be tortured like this every time she gets involved with something."

"I understand."

"And here's a question; how does anyone know it's Vivian talking to her?"

Parkman shifted in the seat and turned his attention to Aaron. "What does that mean?"

"What if the message giver isn't Sarah's sister but someone else? Someone posing as Vivian?"

"What makes you say that?"

"If I were sending messages to my sister, I would not just warn of the impending kidnapping, but also the danger involved. I'd let Sarah know someone was coming, how hard they would attack, and offer ways Sarah could avoid being shot at or dismembered. I mean, really, sending her into burning buildings, getting her beat up, breaking her foot, allowing her to get shot—is that what a sister does? All I'm saying is that I have my doubts about Vivian. The word is too close to *villain*."

Parkman stared at Aaron, his surprise at what he was saying mounting. But at that moment, Parkman understood that much of what Aaron was saying came from a place of pain. He was hurting, already missing Sarah. Aaron hated his decision and wanted to divert some of the blame and responsibility onto someone else, someone safe. Vivian was safe.

"What if Vivian doesn't have that much power?" Parkman asked. "Or that much control? How do we know how hard it is for Vivian, or whoever it is, to communicate with Sarah in the first place? Maybe she can only send out bits and pieces because something governs the information on the other side? Since Sarah has been doing this a long time, let's assume Vivian does have her back. Otherwise, Sarah would be dead by now."

He waited a moment, but Aaron said nothing.

"Does thinking this way make it easier to pull back, pull out?"

Aaron wiped at his eyes but didn't respond.

Parkman watched the flames. The firemen held a perimeter and appeared to have it under control. He tried to examine what made him follow Sarah. Was it the action or the adventure that it added to his life? He knew he loved her as a daughter, a friend, and respected her as a woman, but nothing more, nothing intimate. Maybe it was because of her secret weapon, Vivian, who fought the criminal side of society like no other. He admired Sarah's tenacity. There was no fight too big, no bad guy too strong that Sarah wouldn't step up to first. Parkman hadn't met a single man who would do what Sarah does. And maybe, just maybe, she filled that void in him. The one that wished he had done it differently and damn the consequences. Sarah was more alpha than any man Parkman had ever met.

That's why great leaders were respected and followed because they spoke loud and clear on sensitive issues when not many others would. They fought for what was right and did it with passion in the face of adversity.

Sarah was that kind of girl. She was one of a kind, and Parkman had decided to follow her into the abyss many years ago. That decision had never faltered, never wavered.

Perhaps that was Aaron's issue. He hadn't let go yet. He had to let her go to let her in. He was letting her go now. That was good. He'd be back. Parkman was sure of it.

Once they found her and everything was over, Aaron would make his decision. If he left, there was a chance he wouldn't come back. But if he did, and Parkman suspected he would, then this was just one more step in their evolution as a couple.

But who really knew what was going to happen? Did Vivian? Who even knew if Sarah was dead already or not? If not, where would she end up next?

Parkman suspected only God knew what was in store for Sarah.

And it probably made God nervous.

Chapter 27

The susurrations woke her. She never got seasick or carsick, so it felt odd that she would feel slightly ill from the movement.

The tranquilizer.

She remembered getting a shot while in the back seat of the car. But why was she still swaying, her body weight adjusting left, then right? It was enough that she almost rolled onto her side. She opened her eyes. The small room resembled the lower cabin of a boat. Waves smashed the bow as the boat plowed through rough waters.

She moved to get up but lay back down as a splitting headache flared between her temples. Her hands were cuffed together in front of her. The chain between the cuffs was long enough that she could rub both her temples at the same time. She rested for a moment longer, then tried to get up again, but this time slower. Once seated, she took in the small room.

A toilet sat to her left, enclosed in a small room with a tiny door. On both sides of a table were thin-cushioned seats where food was served and eaten. The bench she had been sprawled out on was close to the door that led outside. Nothing looked like it could be turned into a weapon unless she wanted to cushion someone in the face. She opened a drawer to her left, but it was empty. She opened another. Also empty.

Her head was clearing, the pain subsiding. Even her stomach was settling because hunger now became the issue.

On her feet, she stumbled with the motion of the boat, bumping her shoulder on her way to the door, which was probably locked.

It wasn't.

Upstairs, the sky was blue without a cloud to be seen.

How long have I been out?

She started up the stairs carefully, planting each foot as the boat rose, dropped, smacked the water, and rose again, the engine roaring in the rear, chewing the water as it thrust the vessel forward. Near the top of the stairs, she peeked over the edge. The man steering the boat had his back to her. She recognized him as the driver of the car. The other man he called Frank was nowhere in sight.

She did a full turn to examine the rear of the boat. They were on a yacht and heading out to sea based on the position of the sun. But where were they going? They were far enough that she couldn't see land. She didn't mind swimming, but to swim back from a place where land wasn't visible would be impossible.

She eased higher and saw something that made her stomach drop. A bag of dry cement and a couple of metal pails. A green hose lay spiraled by the pails like a docile snake.

Really? Concrete shoes?

"Hey Frank!" the driver shouted over the wind.

Sarah ducked at the sound of the driver's voice.

"What!" Frank yelled from somewhere behind her.

She moved down a couple of steps. There had to be a way off the boat without having to swim, but the only thing she could think of was to commandeer the vessel. With two armed men and being handcuffed, the odds were stacked against her.

Great, as always, odds I can work with.

"Did you take the picture?"

"Not yet!"

"Do it now, then."

She snuck a quick look. The driver had twisted around to yell over his shoulder. "We'll be there in fifteen minutes."

"Fine!"

Sarah waited on the steps. After a minute, she lifted up again. The driver was gone from the wheel, and the boat was slowing down. She looked behind her. No one.

On the top step, she got a better view of the sea. There was nothing but salt water as far as she could see. They weren't going to an island. They weren't going to meet anyone. This wasn't a new chapter in her life, a new development. This was an ending. Cole had ordered her killed and deposited among sea-going creatures like a common mafia snitch.

"She's awake!" Frank yelled from behind, making her duck her head again.

"Roland!" he yelled. "She's awake."

"Roland?" Sarah said to herself. "The driver's name is Roland?"

Frank stepped around to the front of the stairs and looked down at her. "Knowing our names won't mean anything to you soon enough."

"Just thought his name would be tougher. I mean, he's the alpha male between you two."

"Shut up." He shook his head back and forth. "Making jokes at a time like this. Do you even know where you are?"

"First, I'm not making jokes. I'm serious. He's alpha. You're not. Second, I do know where I am and what you intend to do."

"Oh, really. How's that?" He stepped closer, then dropped down the first step as he slipped a hand behind his back. "You've been in a drugged sleep. How could you possibly know so much?"

Instead of explaining her deductions and how she came to them, she offered him the crazy answer.

"I'm psychic." She rolled her eyes and tilted her head, staring at his face. "You have nice skin." She stared like a lunatic might when thinking about skinning the human head before consumption. Then she righted her gaze, narrowed her eyes, and glared at him. "Psychic. That's how I know shit."

He pulled her Glock from behind his back and aimed it at her. "Get back downstairs. We're not there yet."

"Hey, that's my gun. I want it back." She held out both cuffed hands. "Give it here."

"Shut up. Man, are you ever infuriating. Get downstairs."

"It's probably not even loaded like last time." She smiled wide, showing teeth. When she did, she remembered the backhand at the cottage and rubbed the bottom of her teeth with her tongue. Two felt loose. The mouth movement seemed to mesmerize Frank's eyes.

"What's going on here?" Roland stepped into view.

Frank twisted toward him. "She woke up. Caught her on the stairs. Just taking her back down for her picture."

"There a problem?" Roland asked.

"None."

"Good." Roland moved away and disappeared from sight.

"Do that again," Frank said. "That thing with your tongue."

"What? This?" Sarah rolled her tongue out and around seductively as she watched a transformation come over Frank. It was like hers was the first female tongue he'd seen since spending years in prison or something. His face reddened as he leaned on the railing, lowering the Glock's aim.

"Hey, Frank?" Sarah whispered.

"Yeah?"

"Come join me down here. I might need your help."

"Oh no, you don't," he said. "I'm not stupid. Get in there and lie down on that bed. I have to take your picture."

"Picture? What for?"

"Just move."

He started down the stairs, Glock first. Sarah stepped back until she bumped the door. After fumbling with the handle, she opened it and entered the cabin. At the bed, she sat on the edge.

"Why the picture?" she asked in an attempt to draw the process out.

Vivian, I could use some magic here.

"Lie down," he ordered.

"You won't tell me what the pic is for?"

"No. I'm tired of talking to you."

He seemed gruff now, put out. Like something wasn't going his way.

She eased back and spread out on the thin mattress. Without delay, he lowered the gun, brought the camera up, and took a picture. Then he checked the camera's window.

"Looks good," he said.

"I know what it's for. You're going to Instagram that shit. Tell all your friends you bed me down." She leaned up on an elbow. "You're going to put it on Facebook, too, right?"

He frowned and blew air out of his mouth. "No. You're so stupid. This is to add to our collection. And, it's how we get paid." He started for the door. "Stay down here. We'll come looking for you when we need you. It won't be long now."

"I need your help," she called before he got too far.

He stopped at the door. "What help?"

"I have to pee."

"You'll pee all you want in about fifteen minutes."

"No, I have to pee now." She crossed her legs and drew her hips back as if trying to hold it in. "I feel it coming out."

"Okay, so pee. The toilet's right there."

"I just need your help pulling my pants down." She lowered her head and tried to appear shy, the whole time thinking it wouldn't work. But he slowly turned to face her and then took a step back. "Please, Frank. Come and take my pants off."

"You can undo your pants the way your hands are."

"There's undoing my pants, then my panties, and how do

I use the toilet paper and pull them back up on my own?" She regarded him with sad eyes. "Just help me pee, and then you can head back up, and I'll wait down here like a good girl." She offered a half smile. "You think I like being here? Like this? At least help me use the restroom."

Frank looked over his shoulder and then back at her. "A quick pee. That's all this is? No tricks?"

She swayed her head back and forth. "That's all this is."

Frank set the camera on the table and slipped the gun into the back of his pants. "I'm warning you. Try anything, and I'll lose it on you."

"No tricks." She moved her hands to the side to allow him access to the clasp on her jeans. "Please hurry. Undo my pants, Frank."

He remained cautious, eyes roving her for any sudden movement as he stepped inside her personal space and placed his hands on the clasp. She sucked her stomach in a little to give him better access. After a fumbled attempt, he tried again, and the tightness around her waist lessened.

"Thank you," she said as he stepped back.

Acting like it was hard to push the jeans over her hips with cuffed hands, she looked up at him, her eyes pleading.

"A little help?" She rolled her shoulders inward to appear non-threatening and shy.

Once again, Frank moved closer and eased her jeans down. She stepped out of them, using her feet to stamp the pants down and off her ankles.

"Now, my panties." She positioned herself in front of the toilet room. "Once you ease them down, I'll go, and then pass me some paper. Will you do that for me, Frank?"

He stole a glance back at the door. "Okay, but hurry."

"Get down in front of me and pull my panties off. I'm not modest about my body. You've seen me before out by the cabin when I changed into these clothes. I'm sure you've seen lots of girls before. Just help before I pee all over my only panties." She bounced on the balls of her feet. "Hurry, get down on your knees before me and yank my panties down."

She couldn't believe it when she saw him do it. Frank dropped in front of her, mesmerized by the beautiful woman standing in front of him in her panties, asking him to ease them off. He did exactly as he was told, as any man should, but his actions came with a price this time.

She waited until he kneeled directly in front of her, his arms extended, hands raised to reach her hips. The moment he gripped the sides of her panties and was about to lower them, Sarah drove her right knee into the front of Frank's mouth, driving upward into the base of Frank's nose. A crack accompanied the wet mushy sound as bone met cartilage violently. Frank's head snapped back, but Sarah was already stepping into him again, her right foot rising and dropping, heel first into his face. On the second kick, she almost lost her balance.

Blood smeared across his face. He moaned and rolled to the side, his hand coming around to the gun at the back of his pants. Breathing rapidly now, Sarah collected herself, got into position, lifted her foot above his throat, and dropped it so fast; she hopped up and off the other foot.

Things broke inside Frank's neck. His eyes widened, and his head jerked back, his body wracked with a fit of seizures now. Sarah was horrified with what she was seeing but understood it as necessary. Either she made it to the bottom of the ocean, or they did.

It always had to be them.

His breathing came in fits and starts. Blood slipped from the corners of his mouth and nostrils. His hands fidgeted with convulsions. Then his feet kicked out, and his body stilled, eyes closed.

She heard the last breath as it oozed from his mouth or nose; she couldn't tell. It lasted twice as long as a normal exhale.

"Left with no choice," she said to the corpse, "sorry, but it was you or me. No tricks. This wasn't a trick. This was a treat." She kicked the body. "A picture for your collection? How many girls have you two killed, asshole?"

"Too many," Roland said from the doorway.

By the time Sarah looked up, surprised at the voice, a gun fired in the small room. Wood chunks splintered by her head as she ducked out of reflex. The gun went off again. More wood chunks.

Sarah dove over Frank's body. When she hit the carpet, she slipped her hands into the back of his jeans, retrieved her Glock, and made to turn toward the door when Roland's gun fired again.

The distinctive sound of a bullet entering flesh, the wet plunk, made her sick. She knew she wouldn't feel it for a few minutes, but then it would hurt like a bitch. Maybe even incapacitate her.

The Glock was aimed. Roland backed up in an attempt to slam the door.

Sarah fired anyway.

The bullet took a chunk from the door frame beside his face before he could clear the area. Wood shattered and became airborne.

Roland yelled in pain. The door slammed.

Sarah frantically felt the length of her body for the bullet hole. Confused for only a brief second, she realized that the fleshy sound of a bullet making contact was Frank's body getting hit and not hers.

She flipped him over and searched his pockets for the keys to the cuffs as the boat leaned to and fro, riding the waves slowly, the engine in idle.

Wherever Roland was topside, he wasn't steering the boat anymore. Sarah found a small container close to the back of Frank's belt. She pulled on the clasp and opened it to find two handcuff keys. A moment later, freed from the restraints, she slipped back into her pants, checked the Glock to see that it was ready, and moved toward the door.

She put her ear to the edge and listened. She hadn't heard Roland running anywhere after the door closed. Maybe he just sat in the stairwell, gun ready, waiting for her to open the door. The few windows down here were too small to exit through. It was the door or nothing.

After putting her hand on the doorknob, she eased sideways to get out of the way of a bullet, then shook the knob violently.

Nothing.

Remaining out of the way on the side, Sarah turned the knob until it wouldn't turn anymore, then yanked the door open. It banged against the wall on the other side, then stilled.

Roland wasn't in the stairwell. But there was a little spray of blood. A quick estimate of the location of the blood revealed it probably came from Roland's facial area.

She snuck back to Frank's body, ripped the small container off his belt, and moved back to the open door. She eased up the first step, waited a moment, then tossed the container to the top stair to draw Roland's fire if he was waiting for her.

Nothing happened.

She couldn't sit down here and wait for him but couldn't stick her head up and get shot, either.

She eased up another step. Either Roland wasn't watching the top of the steps, or he was incredibly cool and calm to not have shot at the small container she had just thrown up.

Another step higher. The boat listed from the influence of a wave and then tilted back level.

Sarah thrust her hand above the edge of the stairs.

Nothing happened.

Maybe he wasn't watching the stairs after all.

She placed both feet on the next stair, careful to keep her head below the edge.

Anything Vivian?

She waited a moment, but nothing came.

No news is good news.

Sarah leaped, diving over the last four steps and out into the open. She landed hard on her shoulder, rolled, and pushed herself toward the large steering wheel. No bullets rang out to chase her.

What happened to Roland?

She thrust her Glock out in front of her and frantically searched for a target, but none came into her sights. The top side of the yacht appeared empty.

"Roland," she shouted as she scrambled to her feet and

took cover behind the large wooden wheel. "Where are you? Come on out and talk."

Waiting him out would save her life, but she didn't have a lot of patience. Not knowing where he was pissed her off. They were the only two people on one boat. How well could he hide?

She rose to her feet and scanned the top of the cabin. She would assume she was alone if she didn't know Roland was on the boat. There wasn't another boat in sight, nor land. Only water as far as she could see. But Roland was on the boat. Somewhere. And she couldn't start back toward land until he was dead.

The gun fit snugly at the back of her pants as she started along the side walkway that would take her to the back of the boat, holding tight with both hands to avoid falling into the ocean. As she sidestepped along, her stomach wouldn't let up with the growling reminders of how empty it was. When she was done with Roland, she had to get something to eat.

Holding onto the railing, she traversed the side of the boat, her knees passing the small windows that looked in on Frank's body below. Near the end of the walkway, she slowed, attention riveted on the wide opening at the back where the owners would enjoy cocktail parties and a barbecue.

She waited until the boat listed outward with a large wave, and then as it listed back, she jumped off the side walkway and landed on both feet just inside the railing, the gun out of her pants, up and aimed.

Roland sat on a bench on the other side of the open space, a large white towel stained red pressed to his face. Sarah kept her gun trained on him even though she couldn't see one on him.

"You're hurt bad," she said.

He didn't jump at her voice.

"I'd say so," he said, his voice muffled by the towel.

Sarah sat opposite him and rested her gun hand on her leg, aimed at his crotch directly across the floor of the boat as it rode the waves.

"Frank's dead," she offered.

"I gathered that."

"Why?"

"Why what?"

"Why do what you do? You guys have to know how it'll end."

"I could ask the same question of you."

"Sure you could." A breeze picked up, ruffling her hair. She eased it back off her shoulder with her free hand to let it rest on her back. "But my answer's different because I have an ally on the other side."

"Oh yeah? Did you know that Superman helps me occasionally, but since they've removed many of the phone booths, it's getting harder for him to change." He clenched his teeth, moaned in pain, and said, "So lately, I've been using the Easter Bunny."

"Jokes aside, you're in a lot of pain."

He didn't reply. Nor had he looked at her too well to see the gun.

"I've got my gun back," she said. "And it's aimed at your crotch."

"Good for you." He moaned again, pressing the towel on his face. "I figured as much."

"So tell me, what were your plans?"

"Scare you off."

She leaned back, surprised. "Scare me? I doubt it."

"The concrete was a prop. If we meant to kill you, we would've done it when you were knocked out. Why let you wake up if you were supposed to die out here? What purpose —" He stopped talking as he leaned forward and whimpered, sobbing a little. "Damn, this hurts. I can't believe how fucked up this got."

"Do you work for the dead Dr. Williams or for Cole Lincoln?"

"It doesn't matter who we work for because we don't kill people. We were hired to deliver to you safe and sound. If you die at their hands, that's not on us. We just deliver the goods."

"Well, the delivery's been canceled."

"Evidently."

He sat up, the towel taking on more blood.

She looked out to sea. Still nothing. No boats, no land. She idly wondered what Aaron and Parkman were doing. If they put out the fire at the cabin, they would discover her clothes but not her body. A search party would form. But they'd never think to head out to sea, hours away from the cabin. She needed to get back. She needed to find Cole and end this.

"Where's Cole Lincoln?"

"What's it matter now?"

"Where were you going to deliver me?"

"This is gone too far. It doesn't matter now."

"So tell me."

"Los Angeles."

"Where in L.A.? It's a big city."

"Burbank."

"Burbank? Why there?"

"Not sure, but I understand Cole's something of a movie buff."

"What?" Sarah asked, confused. "How does being a movie buff have anything to do with me?"

He lowered the white towel, now almost completely stained red with blood, and showed her his face. When her bullet had hit the door frame, chunks of wood had shot out. One of them, the size and shape of a butter knife, had pierced his right eye. It had started to swell, the wood still sticking into the center of his eyeball, where blood oozed out and onto his cheek.

"How do I look?" he asked. "Pretty?"

"Sure, if you're auditioning for a Stephen King movie."

"Gee, thanks."

He hadn't answered her question. "What's Burbank got to do with me? Tell me what you know, then I'll turn this boat around, and we can head to Los Angeles to make your delivery. I'll locate Cole and deal with him. You can go to the hospital for that eye wound."

Roland moaned and hitched his shoulders. "I overheard Cole saying he wanted to relive a scene from a movie where James Gandolfini and Patricia Arquette fought to the death in some hotel in Burbank. Some kind of tribute to the late Gandolfini. But what do I care? Even if they fix this," he pointed at the wood sticking out of his eye, "I'll never see properly again. My life is changed forever because of you."

She tightened her grip on the handle of the Glock. When the boat listed over a large wave, she looked out at the empty water around the boat to make sure Roland wasn't diverting her attention from an approaching watercraft.

Roland moved, making her snap her head back toward him, gun raised.

The towel shot sideways. Underneath the blood-stained towel sat his weapon. He had it with him the whole time. He had waited for the chance that she would look away.

His gun fired before she could squeeze her trigger. Then it fired again, almost at the exact moment hers finally did.

She dropped off the bench and sprawled on the floor, firing at him repeatedly until her weapon was empty. Roland dropped his hands to his side, and his head lolled at an odd angle. Three new holes in his abdomen leaked red. Sarah set her gun down and took a deep breath.

"Damn, that was close." She shook her head to clear it. "How the hell did I miss the gun under the towel?"

She got to her feet, thanking her lucky stars that Roland only had one eye, which left him with two-dimensional vision. That would affect the aim of any marksman. The seat where she had been sitting moments before had no holes. His bullets must've been high and wide, where they would eventually drop into the ocean somewhere behind her.

She left her empty gun on the floor of the boat as she walked over and checked for a pulse.

Nothing.

Roland was dead.

She rummaged through his pockets until she located a wallet. Inside, she found a small wad of cash and a spare key to something. Then she flipped the wallet open to the ID and stepped back.

A Los Angeles Police Department picture ID card was inside the small window where regular people would place their driver's license.

"I killed a cop?"

This was bad. She would take heat for this. Even if it was in self-defense, forget that there weren't any witnesses. A Canadian police officer was killed in British Columbia, and Sarah was blamed for it. The media had picked up the story, blasting her picture across the Northern Hemisphere. Later, when it was discovered that she had nothing to do with it, the same media frenzy didn't ensue to vindicate her, which led to trouble with the LAPD when she was trying to help Detective Hirst with a priest killer in L.A. The cops had a hard time trusting her, and now that she had actually killed one of theirs, it would only get worse.

Orders of shoot-on-sight came to mind.

Or was it two cops? Could Frank also be employed by the LAPD?

She jumped up, slipped the cash in her pocket, tossed Roland's wallet into the ocean, and ran along the side railing, careful she didn't fall into the water. Then down the stairs and into the cabin below. Once at Frank's body, she found his wallet, opened it, and examined the ID.

Just as she thought. LAPD Officer Frank Manchelli.

"Shit." She emptied the small wad of cash from his wallet and stuck her head out the door to throw the wallet into the ocean. She looked back at Frank's body.

"Shit. Fuck."

They had intended to deliver her to Cole. They tried to kill her. Both men deserved what they got.

"Dirty cops. Fuck the both of you."

But as for her reputation and ability to remain alive and free from prison, she had to find a way to stop killing cops.

There just couldn't be any more dead cops. Eventually, it would come back to haunt her no matter how innocent she was or justified the kills were.

She grabbed Frank's hands and dragged him to the foot of the stairs. Then, weakening by the second without having eaten, she pulled Frank's body up the steps one by one until she had his body sprawled out on the deck. In the late afternoon sun, the dent in his neck looked horrible. She must've crushed more than his windpipe when she stomped on his throat.

Using what strength she had left, she lifted Frank to the edge and tossed him overboard. He landed with a loud splash and disappeared below the surface, his clothes weighing him down.

After watching Frank sink out of sight, she walked along the side of the yacht until she got to Roland. He was heavier, but she got him over the edge and into the water without much work. Alone on the boat, she headed to the captain's chair, sat down, and used the GPS to move her toward Los Angeles even though she hadn't driven a boat before.

Ten minutes later, the boat cruising almost fifty miles an hour en route for the Los Angeles harbor, Sarah picked up Roland's cell phone, thinking she would call Parkman to reassure him she was okay. Or maybe she should call Aaron.

After a moment of contemplation, she set the phone down. The less anyone knew about her whereabouts, the better. Parkman had friends on the LAPD. She had just killed two of their officers and dumped their bodies in the ocean. She was probably on an LAPD boat of some kind. Maybe she'd call later.

Roland's phone lit up as it rang. She grabbed it to see if

the caller could be identified, but the screen said, private caller.

She set the phone down and let it ring.

Now, more than ever, it was prudent for her to find Cole Lincoln. Deal with him, then meet up with Parkman. He could give her a measure of what was happening, whether the police were looking for her or their two missing men, and then she could make better decisions on what to do next.

As soon as Cole was dealt with, she would be free. Free to make better decisions. Free to work with Vivian. Free of the nightmares and of being haunted by Vivian's memories, which seemed to have abated now that Cole was in her life.

Once she got to Cole and dealt with him, everything would work itself out. Even spending time in jail would be better than being in the same world as Cole Lincoln.

She brushed a tear as it slipped down her cheek. The throttle handle was wet with sweat inside the palm of her hand as she pushed it down. The yacht's engine revved as the bow smacked the waves rapidly like the staccato of gunfire.

The boat cut through the waves.

And Sarah wept.

Chapter 28

Parkman dropped Aaron at the hotel, promising to stay in touch as soon as he heard anything from Sarah. As he pulled out of the hotel parking lot, he called Sarah's parents and discovered they hadn't been contacted regarding any recent developments. Neither of them had heard from Sarah in almost a week. When Parkman hung up with Sarah's father, his phone rang immediately. He looked down, hoping to see Sarah's name.

Nick Kershaw's name filled the screen instead. Parkman approached a red light and answered the call on his hands-free system.

"Yeah, Nick. Learn anything new?"

"There was no body in that fire at the cabin. Her clothes were out front, but who strips in the driveway? It was like someone wanted us to find the clothes, but no Sarah. Which means there's a chance she's alive."

"Okay, but where is she? We have to find her." Parkman accelerated through the green as the light changed.

"Unless Sarah did that herself. Would she burn the cabin to cover something up?"

"Huh? What do you mean?"

"Burned her own clothes. Throw us off her trail."

Parkman thought of something else. "Or throw someone else off her trail."

"Fair enough, but there's something you should hear."

"What?" Parkman applied his signal and pulled to the shoulder of the road. "What is it?"

"Do you know a detective in Los Angeles named David Hirst?"

Parkman stared out the windshield, eyes wide. He took a breath and thought about Hirst and their recent case in L.A. How Sarah almost died in that church fire and then in the hospital and in that car that fell five stories from a parkade—

"Parkman, you still there?"

"Yeah, sorry. What was the question?"

"Detective David Hirst out of L.A. You know him?"

"Yeah, I know him. Old friend of mine. Why do you ask?"

"He called. Said he heard you and Sarah were up in these parts."

"And?"

"He has two missing police officers. Didn't call in like they were supposed to. Haven't checked in with the wives, making them worried wives. You know how that is."

"I do. Why call you?"

"It's weird, but he wants to know if you or Sarah, he said especially Sarah, knew anything about that."

"How would we? She's been kind of busy lately. You know, trying to stay alive and shit."

"I know, and I agree. But you don't find that odd? An L.A. detective loses two cops and calls looking for you and Sarah?"

"Not odd at all. He's a friend to both of us. We helped him with a case. He trusts us. And he knows Sarah can help with these kinds of things. We're just north of L.A., so he probably thought he'd call and give it a shot. Nothing else to it."

"Fair enough. I'll call him back."

"Don't. Let me."

"Done. You call him back then." Kershaw paused. Then asked, "How's Aaron? He holding up?"

"As good as could be. He's at his hotel where he'll wait for word on Sarah."

"Probably the best place for him right now."

"Agreed. Call me back if you get anything on Sarah."

They hung up, and Parkman dialed Hirst right away. While the phone rang on the other end, he adjusted the air conditioning as the late afternoon sun beat through the windshield.

"Hirst here."

"Long time, Hirst."

"Parkman. It is, it is."

"Why call Kershaw? What's up?"

"Since you and Sarah were up that way, I wondered if you'd heard anything about two of my cops that went missing."

"Missing? How does that happen?"

"Abrupt leave of absence. Gone for a week or so.

They're partners. The department didn't like them both leaving at the same time, but they were good men, so the powers that be let it go. Until now."

"What changed?" Parkman asked.

"No calls to the wives in two days. Not answering their cells or their Sat phone. No contact whatsoever. It's like they vanished."

"Why would you call up here?"

"Last we heard, they were headed north of Sacramento. Just checking out areas up that way, and when I heard you and Sarah were near Susanville, I thought I'd put a call in."

Something Aaron had mentioned about the cemetery visit occurred to Parkman at that moment.

"What were they driving?"

"Not sure. Why? You onto something?"

"Find out what they were driving, and I'll tell you what I'm thinking."

"Parkman, I can look it up. Their files are right here. But why the secrecy? It's me, Hirst."

"I know, but I don't want to bark up the wrong tree until I'm sure there's even a tree to bark up."

A cool sweat broke out on his forehead. He changed ears with the cell phone and wiped his brow with his free hand.

"Got it," Hirst said. "Officer Roland Manks drives a black Ford Fusion. That help?"

Parkman lowered his head until it rested on the steering wheel.

"If that's not the biggest coincidence in history, then we might have a problem. A big problem."

"What kind of problem? I'm getting the feeling that I may need to come up there."

“Maybe so. Let me explain.”

Parkman sat up straight, eased the seat back, and told Detective Hirst everything he knew.

Chapter 29

THE SUN HAD GONE down by the time Sarah piloted the boat toward the shore. She entered Marina Del Ray, knowing full well that this boat probably didn't belong there and that it had evidence of a murder on board. Bullet holes, hair fibers, and fingerprints galore. A decent CSI team could lift all the items to discover the previous occupants' identity within a short time.

Had she thought about it earlier, she might've wanted to set the boat on fire and let it sink. But without a lifeboat, she didn't have the energy to swim back to the Los Angeles shore, nor the willpower.

In the still waters, she steered toward the docks, where she found an empty spot on the far side, away from a restaurant that overlooked the boats. She cut the engine and secured the two lines to the dock before jumping back on the boat. In the cabin below, she found a cloth and went about the task of wiping down everything she had touched. It wasn't long before she felt confident she had taken care of any incriminating fingerprints.

Back on land with almost a thousand dollars in cash from the dead cops' wallets, she needed to eat desperately.

Ten minutes later, she was seated in a restaurant by the marina, sipping a glass of zinfandel while she waited for the portobello mushroom chicken and baked potato she'd ordered.

From her pants pocket, she pulled out Roland's cell phone. She stared at it, wondering if Frank and Roland's IDs were real. What if they only had them to get out of jams? Back when she started this crazy business with Vivian, she met a man named Gert. He and his brother carried police ID and presented it to their intended kidnap victims to convince them to come along willingly. Once the victim was missing, witnesses would only claim to have seen police officers picking up the victim.

Maybe Roland and Frank were the same. Enforcers for Cole, with fake police badges to back it up if needed.

Or maybe Roland was telling the truth, and they never intended to hurt her. They could've been working undercover and delivering Sarah to another boat. After that, they would return to Cole and tell him they had killed her.

She had no way of knowing the truth, but there was one way to find out. She could call her only friend in Los Angeles Detective David Hirst.

If it turned out that Roland and Frank were the real thing, it was only right that their families got closure. Hirst knew Sarah. He knew who she was and what she had done for Los Angeles when she redeemed herself with Parkman and the police forces across North America who previously doubted her. Hirst trusted her. When she explained what had happened on the boat, he would know that she acted in self-defense. The boat still had the concrete mix. Roland and Frank's fingerprints would be all over the boat and the concrete bag. Their intent would be obvious. The truth, her story, would convince anyone who took the time to reconstruct the crime scene.

So why did she hesitate to call Hirst? She knew his number by heart. Why not call him to learn if Roland and Frank were real cops?

Maybe it was because she had wiped the boat down. That would show intent to cover up the incident and make her look guilty of something. It would cast suspicion on her needlessly.

So why not call him?

Maybe she was worried that she'd gone too far this time. So far, in all that she had done with her life, killing murderers and rapists never gave her pause, but killing cops, even dirty ones, was not something she wanted to be known for. But that point in time had come and gone. For some reason, lately, dirty cops seemed to be on her radar.

The public understood the death of a child molester and even welcomed it. Or a serial killer. But the murder of a cop in the line of duty, even when Sarah knew he was rogue, was a harder sell.

She set the phone down and decided to wait until after she ate. She needed to think about it some more.

The food came, and she dove in, eating too fast. When she was almost done, she snatched the phone up without another thought, dialed Hirst's private cell, and waited while it rang in her ear. Finally, after six rings, he picked up.

"How can I help you?"

"Hirst?" Sarah asked, her tone deep.

"And this is?"

"This is me hanging up." She pulled the phone away from her ear but hesitated over the end button as Hirst shouted for her to come back. She waited a moment, then placed the phone at her ear.

"Sarah Roberts?" he asked.

"What?"

"Why hang up?"

"Because I called to talk, not play games. When I was here before, you always answered the phone with your name first. What changed?"

"The number on call display. I didn't recognize it."

It dawned on her then. If Roland was a real cop, Hirst might've known the name on call display. There were a lot of police officers on the payroll of the LAPD, so there was a chance he wouldn't know it as well.

But if they were actively looking for Roland …

"Sarah?"

"Yeah?"

"You're here? In L.A.?"

"I'm calling to ask a favor."

"Avoiding my question?"

"This isn't a social call."

"Parkman's worried about you. So is Aaron."

"Tell them I'm fine."

"I just talked to Parkman about two hours ago."

"Oh yeah? What about?"

"We're looking for a couple of missing persons. I heard

you two were near Susanville, so I thought I'd call and see if you'd heard anything about our missing guys."

They were probably looking for Frank and Roland, now deceased, and she was calling Hirst on Roland's cell phone.

Incriminating much?

"Look, Hirst, I'm tied up at the moment, so I haven't got a lot of time."

"Go ahead, Sarah. Why did you call then?"

"I called to ask if you'd relay a message for me."

"To whom and what's the message?"

"Tell Parkman I'm fine, and I'll head to Santa Rosa when I'm done here. He can call Aaron."

"What are you doing here?"

"Private business."

"Then let me ask you a different question."

Sarah didn't want to hear any more questions. She hadn't called to send messages to Parkman but was forced to make it up on the spot. All she wanted to do was get off the phone now. The fine line between doing what was right and good often brought her too close to the criminal side. Her actions could be misconstrued, made to look devious, wrong. The last thing she ever wanted was to be jailed for a decade because of something Vivian had her do that didn't work out. She knew that Frank and Roland had to be killed, or they would've killed her, but killing cops was becoming a habit in a country where cops are known to beat you down for simply not hearing them properly. Videos surface on YouTube all the time. People are shot and killed by cops during a traffic stop or for stealing a can of Red Bull. What would they do to her if they thought she was a cop killer who continuously got away with it? Even if it were just, there would always be a batch of officers who wouldn't believe the defense. This kind of heat only made what she did that much harder. She waited for Hirst's question with bated breath, twirling her fork over the remains of the baked potato.

"I was wondering something, Sarah, and I want a serious answer."

"Go ahead."

"What are you doing with Officer Roland Manks's cell phone?"

The sound of wind came through the tiny speaker.

"Are you in a vehicle?" Sarah asked.

"I'm almost at Marina Del Ray," Hirst said. "We've got two missing cops, Sarah, and suddenly a call comes into my cell from Roland's phone. I had my guys triangulate the call as I wanted to know where the call originated. And wasn't I surprised to hear your voice. So tell me, Sarah, where are Roland and Frank? Or let me ask you a better question. Are they still alive?"

"I'll tell you everything when I come in, not before."

"Then come in, Sarah. Coming in now is the only way."

"No. It. Isn't." She clenched her teeth and breathed out, stabbing the fork into the leftover baked potato. "I have something to finish, and giving you a statement will take too long."

"Sarah, wait for me. I'll help. I'm a friend. Just wait and tell me everything. I know you. I know who you are—"

Sarah cut the call and set the phone down.

"Shit."

She pulled out a few twenties, set them on the table, took a long pull on her wine, then walked briskly from the restaurant. She flagged a passing cab out front, got in, and asked him to take her to Hollywood and Vine.

She knew about the nightclubs there. It was somewhere to disappear for a few hours. Do some thinking. Then she'd catch a cab to Burbank and find a hotel, leading her to Cole, according to Roland.

Somehow, she'd find Cole and end this, with or without Vivian's help.

Up ahead, through the windshield, four police cars led by one unmarked cruiser raced through a red light, headed toward the restaurant she had just left.

She dipped down in the back seat until they had passed.

The feeling that killing two L.A. cops would haunt her longer than Vivian's memories had suddenly become tangible.

A memory could be forgotten eventually.

But cops never forget when you kill one of theirs.

Never.

Chapter 30

P{\scriptsize ARKMAN}'{\scriptsize S} {\scriptsize PHONE RANG AS} he finished dinner at a restaurant near his hotel. When Hirst updated him, he dropped money on the table and stepped outside.

"What?" he said. "That doesn't make sense. Sarah is in Los Angeles and called you on a missing cop's cell phone. I have to tell you, Hirst, that sounds impossible. I wouldn't believe it if I hadn't heard it from you. We're looking for her up here, northeast of Sacramento. L.A.'s almost a ten-hour drive."

"I know. I can't believe it, either. We think she came in on a boat. I've got guys checking the marina now. Otherwise, why eat at a restaurant at the marina."

"For her to be alone now tells me that whoever took her is either heading to a hospital or dead."

"Working on that already. Tell me more about what's happening up there."

Parkman filled him in, leaving nothing unsaid.

"That's one tough girl," Hirst said. "She's been through a lot."

"I suspect she's still going through something." Parkman started across the parking lot toward his car. "Look, I'll head south but won't get there for a while."

"Don't. Get some sleep. Leave early tomorrow and get here for dinner. There's nothing you can do by leaving now and getting here at four in the morning. We'll find her. I'm sure everything will work out."

Parkman stopped at his car and leaned on the trunk. Hirst was right. He needed sleep. He would leave early and get to L.A. around lunch or shortly thereafter.

"Hirst?" Parkman said.

"Yeah?"

"Remember, it's Sarah. Be cool with her. She's not the enemy."

"I know that."

"Seriously. If something happened to those cops, they deserved it."

"That won't go over easy here." A moment later, he said, "If I hadn't met Sarah, we wouldn't even be having this conversation. She'd be a suspect in their disappearance as she was using Roland's phone and refused to tell me how she came into possession of it. When she learned I was coming for her, she bolted. I've got men working the phones trying to see what cab company did a street pickup out here. If she's in a cab, I should know very soon. When I find her, I'll give her the benefit of the doubt, but Parkman, I have to find her, or she has to come in. It's easier if she does it on her own. She doesn't want a dozen LAPD members storming her hotel or wherever she's staying. Things just don't work out the way you want them to when that happens."

"Just do me a favor. Trust that Sarah's innocent. I know I'm right. Give her a chance to prove it."

"I will, and I'll do my best to keep her safe once we find her. But if I don't find her first or she doesn't walk into a police station, I can't guarantee anything."

"I'll be there soon."

Parkman hung up and decided he couldn't wait around. He got behind the wheel and started driving, his bag still in the back seat as he hadn't entered the hotel room after checking in.

Nothing kept him here, and everything made him want to drive all night long to Los Angeles. He started south just as his cell rang again.

Aaron's name came up on the screen. Parkman set the phone back down.

"You wanted out," he said to the empty car. "This is where it starts. Talk to Sarah when this is all over."

The phone quieted after eight rings.

Chapter 31

THE CAB DRIVER SAT in traffic coming along Hollywood Boulevard. Sarah watched people passing by on the sidewalk, seemingly carefree, walking with purpose from place to place. What was it like to be innocent, to go to school, dream of a future, get married, and buy a house? There was so much happening around the tourists and the people of L.A. that they had no idea. They pinballed from the wax museum to the gift shop to the restaurant and then back to their hotel, having no clue that killers were among them.

There were police officers assigned to protect the public who acted contrary to their sworn duty. Wasn't that what this was all about? Cole Lincoln used to be a cop. He broke the law. Evidently enough times that he couldn't stay on as a cop anymore. But being the muscle at a mental hospital in northern California offered him many unwilling victims without recourse.

So maybe in her attempt to stop Cole, her sister had led her to Roland and Frank. Maybe it was just what was needed. And there'd be no blowback on Sarah. She certainly hoped so.

Snapping out of her thoughts, she turned to the driver.

"Would you recommend a good hotel around here?"

He slowed at a red light. "Ahh, how about—"

The phone in her hand rang. It was probably Hirst again, but it came up as a private number.

She leaned forward and thrust the phone over the back of the seats.

"As soon as I hit the button to answer"—it rang again—"I'll put the phone to your ear. Just say yeah or hello. Okay?"

The phone rang a fourth time.

The cab driver nodded. "Okay."

As Sarah reached for the button, she added, "I just want to play a trick on an old friend."

She hit the button and pressed it to the driver's ear as he pulled away at the green light.

On cue, he said, "Yeah," in a deep voice.

Sarah snatched the phone back to her ear and listened.

"Has our guest left this place? Are her shoes heavy, her clothes soaked through yet?"

Cole!

She lowered the mic until it rested on her throat and mumbled, "Mmm, hmm."

The cab was pulling over. She raised a finger for him to be quiet and wait. He put on the four-ways.

"Good, then come to the Safari Inn. I have left your final payment in room 224. Pick up the key at the front desk. Your debt to me has been paid. Let Frank know I appreciate his help, too."

"Mmm, hmm."

The phone clicked off. "Shit." She gazed out the windshield. "Turn around. I need to go to the Safari Inn for the night."

"Safari Inn? The one in Burbank, on Olive Avenue?"

Burbank? Roland had said he wouldn't kill her, but Cole just asked if she was gone. Wasn't Roland supposed to deliver her to a hotel in Burbank to relive a scene from a movie? It had to be the Safari Inn.

"Yeah, that's the one."

The cab driver made a left on Vine and headed away from Hollywood Boulevard and the crowd of tourists taking pictures of the stars on the sidewalk.

Roland had lied. They *were* supposed to kill her on that boat. Bury her at sea. Then the gang in blue just cruise on into L.A. and pick up a payoff and go about their merry way. No one would ever locate Sarah's body, and she would stay missing forever. How many people had this happened to in the past? To have it all worked out, to have it set up so perfectly, meant they must have done it before.

She felt righteous in what she had done to Roland and Frank now. They deserved it. Both of them had followed her to the cemetery. They had attacked her in Dr. Williams's office and again at the cabin. These guys delivered her to Cole before, but Cole wanted her to disappear this time. His fun with her was over. He was ready to move on.

But she wasn't ready to let bygones be bygones.

As the cab sped toward the Safari Inn and room 224, Sarah focused on Vivian, asking if she needed to know anything about the Safari Inn. Was Cole waiting there? Or just a payoff for Roland and Frank? Was she walking into a trap? If Cole wasn't there, where was he?

But all Sarah got in return was silence.

Vivian had been silent in the past, and for good reason. Sarah trusted this was one of those times.

She leaned up and rested her forearms on the back of the front seat.

"If someone threatened you in your cab, what weapons would you use on them?"

"What?" the driver asked, turning to look at her and then back to the road.

She read his name on the cab driver's identification card.

"Mike, I'm not the threat. I just need a weapon. What kind of weapon do you carry, and how much money do you want for it?"

"I have no weapons."

"Sure you do. Come on, I'm a girl. I need one for overnight as I'll be alone in my room."

The driver didn't say anything more as he exited for Barham Boulevard. At a red light, he paused, then took a right-hand turn. Sarah sat back in her seat. She wouldn't push the issue, get him upset, and kick her out of his cab. Stealing the cab would only add to the heat about to come down on her head.

"I have pepper spray," the driver said.

She pushed off the back seat and rested on his again. "How much?"

He seemed to be thinking about it. She looked at the meter. The ride was hitting eighty dollars.

"How about I pay you a hundred and fifty for the ride, and you throw in the pepper spray? Deal?"

He nodded. "Deal. But I don't give it to you until we're parked, and you have paid me."

"No problem."

She watched the lights of the Warner Bros. Studio as the car passed it on the right.

Now she was going into room 224 with a weapon. That's all she ever needed. A fighting chance.

Chance favored the prepared mind, but was she prepared?

Chapter 32

DETECTIVE HIRST DROVE HIS cruiser hard, taking corners recklessly, a single red light rotating on the dash, no siren. Things were moving fast. One of his tech guys was able to track the phone to Hollywood Boulevard but then lost the signal. Meanwhile, Hirst had an officer calling the cab companies who had cars in the Marina Del Ray area looking for a driver who picked up a lone girl matching Sarah's description from the restaurant.

He was five minutes away from Hollywood and Vine when his phone rang again. He pressed the hands-free button.

"Hirst here. What have you got?"

"The cab."

"Talk to me."

"Yellow cab. Driver picked up a girl in front of the restaurant. Drove her to Hollywood Boulevard and then dropped her at a hotel in Burbank."

Hirst slammed on his brakes and checked his mirrors to make a U-turn.

"What hotel?"

The last car in a row passed him. He spun the wheel, turned the other way, and hit the gas, heading to the 101 Hollywood Freeway. A moment later, he passed the two cruisers that had been following him. In the mirror, he watched as neither one did a U-turn to follow him.

"Driver said she asked him to stop two blocks from the Safari Inn, but she might've been going to the Coast Hotel, which is right beside it."

"Anything else?"

"The guy said she bought his pepper spray. Said she needed a weapon."

"Got it. That it?"

"Yup."

He ended the call and whacked the steering wheel with his open hand.

"Dammit, Sarah, what are you up to?"

Then he speed-dialed Parkman, who answered on the second ring.

"I thought you'd be asleep," Hirst said.

"Can't. On the road. Heading south to you. What's up?"

"Sarah's in trouble."

"I figured. How much trouble?"

"She took a cab to a hotel in Burbank and bought the driver's pepper spray. She's up to something. I've got officers en route. I'm heading there myself."

"How far away are you?" Parkman asked.

"Ten, maybe fifteen minutes."

"Who's going to get there first? You or the LAPD?"

“Me.”

“Good.”

“Parkman, you better get down here. Something tells me Sarah’s going to need a friend.”

“I’m on my way.”

“Just hurry.” Hirst ended the call as he used the ramp to get on the 101.

Then he tried Roland’s cell number. If Sarah would answer, he could warn her. Talk her out of whatever it was she wanted to do.

He pushed the car to over eighty miles an hour when she didn’t answer.

Then he hit the siren.

Chapter 33

When the bright sign of the Safari Inn came into view, Sarah told the cab driver to pull over two blocks short of the hotel. She paid the driver, took the pepper spray, and exited the vehicle. As the door slammed, the driver's phone rang, and she moved into the darkness along the side of the road. The cab pulled away slowly as the driver was on his phone. A moment later, it disappeared around a corner and was gone.

Up one side of Olive Avenue was a McDonald's, still open, vehicles lined up in the drive-through. The other way was only darkened windows in storefronts.

One man walked in the opposite direction with a dog on a leash.

She headed away from the hotel until she came to a street light. When the light changed, she crossed the street to the Safari Inn side, then turned toward it. Slowly, her hands wrapped around the small canister of pepper spray, she moved along the sidewalk until she stood in front of the Coast Hotel doors, a small hotel half a block from the Safari Inn.

Roland's phone rang. She jumped at the sound and pulled it out. Hirst was calling again. The phone wasn't needed for where she was going. As best she could, she wiped the phone of prints, flipped it to vibrate, and then tossed it in the bush beside the front doors of the Coast Hotel. If Hirst followed the phone's signal, he would be at the wrong hotel.

Sarah continued up the street and walked purposely in front of the Safari Inn until she had passed it, staying on the sidewalk. She continued until bushes obscured her view of the hotel. At the next corner, she turned left to walk behind the building. The entire time, nothing seemed out of the ordinary. No car had occupants sitting, watching the hotel. The clerk had been playing solitaire on a computer behind the counter. One guest was unpacking the trunk of his car into a ground-floor room as Sarah walked by. In front of another room, men stood around motorcycles, beers in hand.

At the back of the hotel, no doors offered access to the rear of the rooms. The only way in was the front. Room 224 was on the second floor. The Safari Inn was only two stories high, and an outside stairwell and a walkway accessed the second-floor rooms.

To stand outside the room would be dangerous. To knock on the door, having no idea what was behind it, was also dangerous. But she had to admit, hunting Cole had been dangerous from the start. Nothing had really gone well for her, but here she was, without any idea what she would find in room 224 and with no other option but to move forward.

She turned back to the front of the hotel. The only way to

do this was to knock on the door as Roland's messenger. If someone was in the room, the story would be that she works for Roland, and he felt it was safer for her to come than for him. She was to pick up whatever Cole left behind. Cole had no idea that Roland was languishing in the ocean hours away. The only danger to Sarah was if Cole had decided Roland and Frank were to be killed, which meant room 224 was a trap.

But she had no other choice.

Before taking the stairs, she stopped to watch as a pickup truck backed up to the open door of a room on the first floor. The driver expertly maneuvered between two Harley-Davidson motorcycles. He cut the engine, got out, yanked the tailgate down, grabbed a case of beer, and walked into the room's open door. She was close enough to hear him tell the others in the room that he would go back out for more beer shortly.

None of these people had anything to do with her. This looked increasingly like Cole had sincerely dropped a payment off for his hired cops.

She started up the stairs cautiously. She leaned over the railing on the second floor and looked out at the pool, taking it all in, watching for movement. Traffic on Olive Avenue was light at this hour. Another Harley pulled in, cruised the lot, and then the rider pulled up to the other bikes and walked it back to park beside the pickup truck. He cut the engine, dismounted, and pulled off his helmet, leaving it on his bike seat. She missed her bike. The days of riding for hours, no messages, no notes. And no Cole Lincoln. The noise in the room grew when the new rider entered, then simmered down until it was a dull din.

Satisfied no one watched her, she nonchalantly strolled along the second floor. She passed 228, then 226, paying close attention to the blinds in the little windows. Then she came up to 224 and, without slowing, passed it, too. Nothing out of the ordinary happened. No noise, no movement, nothing. It was as if she was lost and simply looking for her hotel room. She kept going until she reached another stairwell.

"This is maddening," she whispered under her breath. "Am I walking into a trap?" she asked Vivian.

No answer came. Silence accompanied her thoughts. Vivian's new internal voice remained quiet.

The time to stake out the place was over. Detective Hirst and half of the LAPD were probably on their way here. She had used Roland's phone. Hirst wanted answers. Answers she didn't want to supply or wouldn't right now. Time was not just running out; it was gone.

She strode up to room 224, flipped the safety off the lip of the pepper spray, and knocked on the door, keeping her body to the left. In the parking lot below, nothing moved. While she waited, breathing slowly to remain calm, she listened for any movement behind the door. All she heard was the dim sound of revelers below. No one answered the door. She knocked again, harder. Then she tried the door. It was unlocked. On the count of three, she turned the knob and pushed the door open with force. Before the door swung back and closed on its own, she caught a glimpse of a briefcase on one of the double beds of an otherwise empty room.

With her back to the wall beside the door, she breathed in deeply, scanned the area below the walkway once more, and decided to enter.

The door opened with ease. She slipped inside and placed her back against the wall while she waited for the door to close.

She lowered to the carpeted floor and looked under the beds. It was clear to the far wall. In this small hotel room, the only place left to hide was the bathroom or the armoire.

If someone were in the room, they would know someone else had entered it by now. Since no one had jumped out when she opened the door and still heard nothing, Sarah began to think she was alone and that this wasn't a trap unless Cole had the room wired to blow.

As soon as that thought hit her, a chill made her shiver. That was Cole's style. He had figured out a way to burn down the mental hospital by starting a fire in her room and making it look like she had done it. Cole had been intimately involved with fire in the past—his facial scarring carried the evidence. He had probably ordered the cabin to burn down. Everything regarding Cole had been about burning things, so it would make sense if this room was set to blow. He hadn't rigged it to the door opening. So how? Maybe when the briefcase was opened. Or moved. But wouldn't Vivian have warned her?

Quickly, she cleared the wardrobe cabinet, and then, holding the pepper spray canister out front, she examined the restroom, pulling the shower curtain back.

The hotel room was empty.

It could simply be a drop, after all. Would Cole even take the risk of terminating LAPD officers? But if it was only a payment drop, then Cole was gone. When would she ever catch up to him again?

She sat on the bed closest to the bathroom and stared at

the briefcase. This fight seemed to be out of her hands the whole time. When would it end? When would Cole be at her mercy instead of the other way around? He may have his friends and his favors, but she had Vivian. No one was a match for Vivian. But her sister had gone through a quiet period again, leaving Sarah on her own. What was that all about? She needed a way out of this. The LAPD was missing two members. Sarah was going to be suspect number one. And how unfortunate for her that she was the one who killed them. There was no easy way out of this. No obvious solution.

"Unless you've got something up your sleeve, sis?" she whispered.

Get behind the bed. Up against the wall.

Vivian's thought rang through Sarah's head like a distant echo in a mountain range. Those eight words reverberated over and over, dimming in volume as they went.

Sarah reacted instantly. She twisted to the side and dropped behind the bed as instructed. She wiggled around until she had eyes on the base of the door, the canister in her hand held tight.

A car screeched to a halt outside. A door slammed shut. She waited. Voices outside. A man shouted something about a door.

What's that all about? The biker's party?

Someone ran by the room. Footsteps stopped in front of the door. Someone knocked. She waited, her heart pounding in her chest. Breathing through her mouth helped regulate her heightened alertness as her palms moistened.

The knob turned. The door opened. A set of black shiny dress shoes entered the room and stopped, the door propped open.

"Sarah?" Detective Hirst said.

After working closely with him recently, she recognized his voice but stayed where she was. Vivian wouldn't have told her to hide if he weren't a threat.

"Sarah? I know you're in here. What's the briefcase for? Runaway money?" There was a moment of silence. "You didn't turn the phone off. I found it in the bushes next door. The cab driver told me he dropped you off two blocks away, but you told him the Safari Inn in Burbank. He knew where you were going. The front desk clerk looked away from her computer game long enough to tell me she saw you enter this room. Room 224. So come on out and talk to me."

She breathed through her mouth, waiting. The music from the room below increased in volume. Someone shouted a rowdy salute.

She could probably trust Hirst, but trust went out the window when a cop thought you had something to do with the death of one of theirs. She was putting all her money on Vivian, and it was Vivian who had told her to hide.

"Sarah, c'mon, I can help. Tell me what happened to Roland and Frank. Let's put this behind us. People will understand. You've done a lot of good. If it was self-defense, not only will we get this monkey off your back, I'll personally get involved. I'll get you a good lawyer." He stepped farther into the room. "Parkman and I will be with you every step of the way."

The noise below increased another notch.

Any other pearls of wisdom, Vivian?

To see if Hirst held a weapon, she would expose her position. But he was bound to find her soon enough anyway.

He stepped closer again. Another step. Hirst stopped at the briefcase. A loud metallic click signaled the undoing of one of the clasps on the case.

"Sarah? What are we doing here? Come out of the bathroom. Show me what's in the case."

Another click.

Then someone in running shoes stepped into the doorway. This person moved quietly and fast. They pulled on the door and let it shut.

Hirst's shoes twisted on the carpet as he pivoted to look at who had entered behind him.

Sarah couldn't suppress her startled short yell as a gun fired in rapid succession. It felt like it went on forever, but when it stopped, she counted at least six shell casings on the floor by the man in the running shoes. Small puffs of drywall dust floated down and landed on and around her.

Hirst made a weird sound, a gurgling. The bed she hid behind shook with his weight. Then he slipped off and hit the floor, his eyes wide in terror and pain. Blood spilled from his leg and his stomach. Their eyes met. In that glance, she saw him warn her to stay hidden. More blood covered his chest, but it took her a second to see it came from an arm wound.

She now knew why Vivian got her to hide and stay hidden.

Hirst grunted as he was pulled onto his back. The man wearing running shoes stood over him.

"You stupid idiot," Cole said.

Sarah's jaw clenched, and she let air out through a small hole she formed with her lips as she listened to that voice, one she would never forget. A feeling, part fear, part elation, came over her. Cole Lincoln was here. No more hunting him, hoping to catch up. He was here. He was hers. But she was still at a disadvantage. She had brought a canister of spray to a gunfight.

"You almost opened the briefcase," Cole said. "Do you realize the damage you would've caused? I can't have Sarah killed that way. Isn't that right, Sarah? You were meant to die in the fire at the Amy Greg Hospital, but you escaped." He stepped toward the other bed. "I'm still shaking my head as to how you did that. Ingenious, really. But how you escaped Roland and Frank is beyond me. They were supposed to bury you at sea." He picked something up off the other bed. The noise from downstairs grew louder still. "The bomb in that briefcase would've blown Roland and Frank apart. I didn't need them anymore. My time on the force is long over. The favor they owed me has been paid in full." He was standing over Hirst again. "But I don't understand why you're not dead yet, Sarah. How could you get out of that room in the hospital? How did you get back to L.A. on Roland's boat? How did you, a little girl, overpower two armed police officers?"

A pillow landed on Hirst's chest. He was breathing in fits and starts as he bled on the carpet. She had to do something, or he would die in room 224 of the Safari Inn.

"I guess I have to kill you myself," Cole said. "But I'm willing to make it quick. Think of it as a favor to you. After all, you eliminated Dr. Williams for me. You took care of Roland and Frank. All I have to do is finish this guy and then help you to your meeting with God, and I'd about call us square. Sound good to you?"

Hirst pushed the pillow off and tried to roll over. From under the bed, Sarah watched as Cole dropped to his knees, grabbed the pillow, and forced it over Hirst's face. Hirst squirmed and moaned, but the pillow muffled the sound. And he didn't fight back with anything matching Cole's strength as the bullets in his body had sapped him.

Hirst would die if Sarah stayed where she was. Then she would die. When bullets sprayed the room, Vivian had gotten her behind the bed and saved her life. But lying on the floor behind the bed was over. She took a deep breath, pushed off the floor, got her feet under her, and dove up and over the edge of the bed.

Cole saw her coming. He released the edge of the pillow with his gun hand and brought the weapon around to aim, but wasn't fast enough as Sarah landed on him. She came in hard, her shoulder driving into his cheek, slamming his face into the dresser unit that held the TV.

They wrestled over Hirst in a jumble of arms and legs. The gun exploded beside her. She jumped at the sound and then grabbed the arm holding the weapon to gain control over it. Whether she was hit or not wouldn't save her life. She focused on getting that gun to stop spitting death pills.

Cole forced her down, the gun coming with her, slowly getting closer. She redoubled her efforts, now wedged between Hirst and the dresser. She thought back to what Aaron had taught her. About the distribution of weight and using her opponent's weight against them. She paused a moment longer until Cole pushed down with both hands, his shoulders locked, his face intensely screwed up, that ugly burn mark making him look grotesque.

Then she let go of all resistance, twisted sideways so the gun would smash into the carpet, and brought her legs up to wrap around Cole's waist as he fell forward. Behind his back, her feet wrapped and locked at the ankles, and before he recovered, she locked him down in a scissor hold. Then, careful to aim accurately, Sarah pummeled him with her fists about the jawline and below, aiming for the soft spot in his throat.

Cole abandoned the weapon in his defense, bringing his hands up to block the punches while trying to catch a breath as his diaphragm was being crushed inward. He pushed up off the dresser, but Sarah came with him, locked to his abdomen. He tried again, pounding at her legs, but she refused to let go. His face reddened, but he fought on. She pushed off the dresser and did a half sit-up, then jabbed three times at his teeth and nose, her legs still firmly planted around him.

It was only a matter of a minute left. He couldn't hold on breathing the way he was. She had him. She would finally stop him. She only hoped Hirst was still alive. He had heard an explanation of Roland and Frank's death from the man who tried to kill him. Sarah could move on, free from the dark clouds Cole had brought into her life. But it didn't look good for Hirst. And there was that other bullet the gun had spit out that she hadn't accounted for yet.

Cole bucked her, lifted up, bringing Sarah with him, then smashed her back to the floor, rattling her teeth when she hit.

He reached up in a last-ditch attempt to get her off him, grabbed the edge of the TV, and pushed it toward her. The TV crashed down and landed on her chest. She brushed it off, but her legs weakened a notch in the effort. Cole raised a hand, formed a fist and a smile, then brought the fist down into Sarah's groin. Because of the angle of the scissor hold, the fist smashed just inside her hip bone.

She shrieked, her head back as the pain was instant, sharp, and crisp. It felt like a tendon gave up and announced its retirement from all the abuse it had undergone. She screamed again and tried to tighten her grip, but her legs wouldn't respond in the same way, weakened by the blow. Cole dropped his fist again, and her scissor hold around his waist loosened, then fell off.

Instead of attacking her, Cole grabbed his gun and got to his feet.

"Stupid bitch," he gasped. "You need to die."

He aimed the gun at her face and pulled the trigger.

It clicked empty. In that second, Sarah froze, sure a bullet would rearrange her features. The empty click propelled her to crawl backward, roll away and get to her feet. When she turned around, Cole was running from the room.

"Cole!" she yelled, but then he was gone.

She dropped to one knee and checked Hirst's pulse. It was weak, but she felt it.

"Get," Hirst said. "Him." Then he coughed.

Sarah grabbed the phone in the room and hit zero to get to the front desk.

"Safari Inn," the clerk said. "How can I help you?"

"An LAPD officer is dying from multiple gunshots in room 224. Call everybody. Get someone here. Save his life!" She slammed the phone down.

"They're on their way, Hirst. I gotta go."

She thought she detected a nod but wasn't sure. Once out the door, she looked both ways. Cole was no longer on the second floor. At the railing, she looked down. He was jumping into the pickup truck directly below. The same one, the guy with the beer, came in. She remembered the guy was supposed to go back out for more beer.

He wouldn't leave the keys in the ignition—

The pickup started with a cough and a rumble. It clunked as Cole dropped it into gear.

Sarah used the railing as leverage, hopped, and swung her legs over the edge without thinking. Then she let go and dropped the twelve feet to the bed of the pickup. Her knees buckled upon landing, her shoulder taking the brunt of the fall as the back of the truck planted a hard kiss on her cheek. The kind that would leave a massive bruise. She opened and closed her mouth to make sure nothing in her face was broken as she flipped over to look in the back window of the cab.

Cole watched her. He smiled. Then he waved.

The engine revved loud. She went to grab onto something, but he released the brake, and the pickup shot forward. Sarah tumbled over and over until she passed the edge of the tailgate and dropped a few feet to the concrete of the parking lot. In some ways, that hurt more than falling into the back of the truck. The concrete was hard and unforgiving. It rattled her teeth and made her face feel even more numb.

She spun around and got up on one knee to watch Cole hit the entrance to the parking lot and screech onto Olive Avenue, going left, away from Los Angeles. Her eyes locked on the Harleys, checking for keys. None had them.

The room under hers was still loud. None of the partiers inside noticed their truck had just got stolen. The music thumped as Cole drove away.

A leather-clad biker stepped outside, walked by without casting a look her way, and grabbed a small leather case from one of his saddlebags.

His keys jangled from a belt loop.

Sarah sprang into action. She stepped closer, grabbed his keys, and yanked them forcefully off, ripping the belt loop.

"Hey, what the—"

She stepped into the back of the biker's knee, then pushed, so he fell away from her and the bike.

Without pause, she hopped on the bike, flipped through the few keys on the chain, and fired up the Harley. Anxious that Cole was a mile away already, she dropped the Harley in gear and tore from the parking spot just as the inebriated biker was getting to his feet.

She hit Olive and drove into traffic without looking, but at this hour, it was light. A wide arc brought her into the right lane, where she opened the bike up, skirting a blue car, then a black Caddy.

Ahead, a light changed to yellow. But she kept the bike going, looking for the pickup truck. People were crossing the road toward a Starbucks on the right. Sarah steered left, then dropped the bike to the right at the last second and slipped between the pedestrians as they tried to jump away.

The road opened up after that, but Cole could've gone anywhere. Any road on either side would facilitate an escape route. He could be long gone, and she would never find him again unless Vivian wanted to help, but she'd been almost useless lately.

The wind pulled her hair straight back and massaged the skin on her cheeks. She narrowed her eyes as they watered, staring at the taillights ahead.

Then she saw him.

The same pickup. Stopped at a crosswalk.

What a fucking idiot. Who stops at a crosswalk when

they're on the run?

She slowed the bike enough to maintain control and to get close to the pickup without spooking him. The brake lights dimmed as Cole, and the two other vehicles that had stopped started moving again.

All Sarah could do was follow him. She had no weapons, and she couldn't smash into him with a Harley Davidson. She would ruin the bike and probably kill herself.

Another light was coming up, but it was still green. She watched the back of Cole's head and waited for him to recognize her.

"Come on, Vivian, help me out here. I can't follow him all night."

Sarah was close enough to see Cole's face in the mirror as he leaned up to check it. He must've thought he was free and clear. In a stolen pickup, he could dump anywhere. The cop was shot and bleeding, probably dying. Sarah had fallen out of the back of the pickup.

"But here I am. Surprise, surprise, asshole."

The pickup jerked forward as he slammed the gas down. Sarah charged after him.

The light up ahead turned yellow. The pickup dropped a gear and surged forward, racing for the yellow. Then the light flipped to red, and Cole was still at least fifty yards away.

Sarah kept up. She wasn't about to lose him again. At the thirty-yard mark, she was almost beside him. He jerked the pickup toward her. She anticipated the move, dropped the bike to the side, and crossed the center line, but the lanes were empty as the red light ahead stopped them. She righted the bike as they both came up to the intersection. A glance to her right confirmed he was still with her, watching to see if she would crash the Harley, but after years on her BMW bike, she handled the Harley expertly.

Ahead, the intersection was quiet. But Sarah was out far enough on the left to see the large eighteen-wheeler as it entered on the green light, blocking Cole's path. There was only enough time for her to look over at Cole before she bailed from the bike. Cole still had his eyes on her.

She lifted her leg to avoid being crushed as she dropped sideways and let the bike slide ahead, out from under her. Cole must've realized what she was doing and turned to look ahead. Tires screeched as he hit the brakes. She didn't have time to look as she slid on her butt under the rig, its hulk rushing above her. She missed the back of the cab's tires by half a foot. By the time she slid out on the other side, a wicked-sounding crush of metal on metal told her that Cole had rammed the back of the rig with the pickup.

Sarah rolled off her butt as it started to burn and came to a stop ten feet past the rig. She gasped for breath at how close that was and stared up at the large truck. It had stopped and was just settling back after being hit with enough force to tilt it momentarily.

The pickup's tires were easy to see under the rig, but something was odd about them. The back tires were almost touching the front ones. The pickup had buckled on impact. Steaming liquid squirted out of the pickup, hissing where it touched the pavement. Smoke enveloped the area where the hood once was. People started to gather on the other side of the rig. Two men approached her, one asking if she was all right. Sarah overheard someone on the other side of the rig saying, "I saw the whole thing. They were drag racing."

She got up on her elbows, took a deep, calming breath,

and pushed off the pavement to sit up on her knees. The world spun for a moment, her heart still racing. Something made a snapping sound on the pickup side of the rig. Flames emerged from under the hood. People on that side stepped back. Someone yelled that it was going to blow.

The two men who had approached her grabbed each arm and started pulling her back.

A small explosion rocked the rig back and forth. Then another, and the men holding her stumbled, but they held on. When she looked back, from what little she could see, what was left of the pickup was engulfed in flames. There was no way Cole had gotten out in time. The way the pickup had buckled, the driver's seat would've been smashed into the side wall of the rig.

"Burn, bitch, burn," Sarah mumbled as the men set her down on the grass beside the road.

"What's that?" one of them asked.

Sarah lay down and stared up at the stars in the sky. It was over. It was truly over. Cole Lincoln was dead. Her nightmare memories from the past could have closure. They could be put away now, healed.

Vivian's memories that had haunted her seemed to have cleared up as well. It felt like a fresh start.

As long as Hirst stayed alive, though. Hirst was her get-out-of-jail-free card because he heard everything Cole had said. He heard how Roland and Frank were working for Cole and how they were sent to kill her. Hirst would corroborate everything.

Her eyes closed. It felt good to rest. To just lie under the stars and not move. Everything seemed to ache and protest. She was getting older in a young person's business.

At the sound of sirens, she forced herself to sit up. Police cars roared in, followed by a firetruck and paramedics. She craned her neck to look at the pickup. It was engulfed in yellow and orange flames.

She felt sadistic with pleasure, but the bastard deserved to die by fire.

"It's called karma, and it's pronounced, *eat shit*. The asshole, the asshole, the asshole is on fire. Let the motherfucker burn."

"What's that?" someone said beside her.

The briefcase is in the motel room.

She forgot about the briefcase. If a careless cop entered room 224 and opened the case, it could blow the room up with Hirst in it.

She had to get back to the Safari Inn.

She braced herself to get up and stood on wobbly legs.

"Where do you think you're going, Miss?"

Sarah turned to look at who was talking to her. Two police officers had stepped up behind her.

"I have to get back to the hotel."

"You won't be going anywhere right now, Miss. You need to see a paramedic, and we need to talk to you about what happened here."

She leaned in close to one of the officers. "If we don't return to the Safari Inn right now, people could die. There's a bomb in room 224. Call the bomb squad. Have them remove it, then. But call it in. Deal with it."

The other officer stepped up, pointing his finger. "Hey, I recognize you. You're that girl who helped with the priest killings. Sarah, something."

"Sarah Roberts and you have to listen to me. Detective

David Hirst will die if that bomb goes off. He's been shot three times, and he's in the room that asshole," she pointed at the burning pickup, "left a bomb in."

The cop who knew her name pulled out a cell phone. "What hotel again?"

"The Safari Inn. Hurry!"

He dialed out. "The one just down here, on Olive."

"The same."

The explosion in the distance made everyone duck, even though the Safari Inn was quite a few blocks away. Sarah hobbled around the cab of the large rig. The fireball was huge like an F-16 had dropped a guided missile in the center of Burbank.

Hirst was dead. And many other innocent lives as well. Cole would get the last laugh, after all. It was over. She had no idea how to talk herself out of this mess now that the only person who could help explain what had happened with the missing cops had just died in a ball of flames.

She looked skyward, her eyes watering.

Thanks for this, Vivian. You've been a real sport.

The street sign caught her eye. She was standing at the intersection of Olive Avenue and Victory Boulevard.

Victory Boulevard.

How ironic.

Chapter 34

Interview Room Seven, or IR7 as the detectives referred to it, was rather splendid compared to other interrogation rooms Sarah had frequented in the past. After six hours, four coffees, two sandwiches, and lots of water, she had offered the men and women investigating the hotel, chase, and car accident incidents her statement, telling her side twice. No one asked her about the disappearance of Roland or Frank, which she was thankful for but was beginning to worry about. Why wouldn't they? When Hirst was following her after using Roland's cell, chasing her with cruisers in tow, why not question her on why she had Roland's phone? Unless Hirst had kept that to himself. And who was the guy she had been chasing? They weren't very interested. All they wanted was her version of the events, and when the questioning strayed off the events of the Safari Inn and the crash at Victory Boulevard, Margot, the female detective who seemed to be in charge, reined them back in to keep things on track.

Maybe they found Roland's phone or parts of it in the debris at the hotel and assumed Hirst had done something rogue and died for his efforts. Whatever the reason, she wasn't prepared to open Pandora's box by bringing up the subject.

As everyone filed out of the room, Margot stayed behind. She leaned against the closed door, pulled out a business card, and fidgeted with it, sliding it under her fingernails to clean them. Her misty gray eyes were unreadable—a good trait to have when interrogating.

This could go one of two ways. One, they had allowed Sarah to tell her story, which wasn't the whole story, letting her trap herself before they were to charge her for the murder of two LAPD officers. Throw her to the lawyers and judges and let the courts figure it out.

Or two, this was over, and for some reason, they were about to let her go.

That was the maddening part. She couldn't read Margot. The smile on the detective's face was either a knowing smile like I got you now or an admiring one.

"Sarah?" Margot said.

Sarah uncrossed her hands and allowed her body language to be open without responding.

"You telling us everything?" Margot asked.

"If I'm not?" Sarah asked back, waiting for the, *or else*.

Margot looked up from the business card, tossed it on the table, and opened the door.

"Take the card. Call me if you think of anything else. But stay close for a few days. There are more statements to go through." She paused for a moment, then met Sarah's gaze. "We lost a lot of bikers at that motel. But hey, that's greed for you."

That was the first time anyone spoke of the bomb or its casualties. Even though it appeared that Margot was letting her go and not charging her with anything, Sarah remained seated.

"Greed?"

Margot shrugged. "It's sad, but that's the nuts and bolts of it."

"I'm missing something."

"After you left the room, the bikers came upstairs to see where the girl came from who stole their bike. They were probably hunting for blood. The state detective Hirst was in must've startled them. Emergency services were already en route. Hirst talked them into carrying him out of the room, wounds and all. He wanted as far from that briefcase as possible."

The only way Margot could know all this was through the statements of others, as Hirst most surely died in the explosion. But if he had been carried out before the explosion, Sarah wondered if Hirst might be alive.

Margot moved into the room and braced her hands on the back of the chair opposite Sarah. "These guys, with Hirst bleeding out from three gunshot wounds, carried him all the way to the front desk where paramedics were arriving. Then they headed back to the room to look for clues to who you were. Half a chapter of the L.A. Riders spilled into room 224 to decide what to do to the chick who stole their bike when one of them opened the briefcase."

"Oh, no."

"Exactly." Margot pushed off the chair and opened the door to Interview Room Seven again. "You won't have to worry about biker gangs coming after you. The media got wind of the story and twisted it to look like a biker war with the only one making it out alive was some biker chick who slid under the rig that killed the guy chasing her."

Sarah nodded. This was good. She couldn't write it this well.

"So let's leave it at that," Margot added.

Sarah got up from the table. She didn't need to be asked twice. At the door, Margot grabbed her arm.

"Cool?"

Sarah nodded. "Let's leave it at that," she repeated.

"Good. Now, you're going to need a ride."

"A ride?"

They stepped out into the hallway.

"Of course. The hospital is a bit of a walk from here."

"I can only assume you're taking me to see Hirst?"

"If he's out of surgery, the doctor will let us in. He asked for you before going into surgery. Said you saved his life. Something about jumping the guy. Hirst said he was sure you would eat a bullet for him. He said that if you made it, he wanted to see you when he woke up in the ICU." Margot was shaking her head. "Wait until I tell him you stole that Harley and almost died going after the perp."

As Margot talked, a feeling of elation akin to freedom overwhelmed Sarah. Hirst was alive. He didn't die, and no one told her. Hirst knew she was innocent. Hirst trusted her and saw what she did for him. Things would work out after all.

They started down the hallway, Margot in the lead.

"Oh, and a man named Parkman is at the hospital. He came here first. Asked for you, but you were busy with us. Said he'd wait with Hirst. Funny guy, though."

"Why funny?"

"He had a toothpick in his mouth like he just had a steak, and he wouldn't offer another name. Just Parkman. Who has only one name?"

Sarah smiled.

Those toothpicks. He probably found a flavored one.

"Parkman is only known by one name," Sarah said. "I've never heard another for him. Maybe one day I'll ask about that."

It felt like a palpable weight had been lifted. She followed Margot to an unmarked LAPD cruiser with a lighter step.

Chapter 35

ON THE WAY TO the hospital, Margot drove without talking. They had said enough in room seven. It gave Sarah a chance to reflect and make peace with Vivian.

For the first time in days, Vivian's presence was close by. Sarah felt her intimately close, lingering inside her head, listening to Sarah's thoughts, a feeling still somewhat foreign but welcoming.

The knowledge Vivian imparted to Sarah in a flash was that Vivian's memories would stop now. The horrid images would disappear and cease to come back, but Vivian couldn't help what was already there. Now that Cole was dead, Sarah could move on as well. But she would have to do it without Aaron.

Sarah wiped a tear away before Margot could see it when Vivian made her aware that Aaron was already in Toronto. He headed back when Parkman got to L.A. and told him

Sarah was fine. She wasn't even in the hospital. Only scrapes and bruises this time. Aaron was supposed to head to Toronto anyway, but leaving this way still hurt. She was supposed to call him. They could talk. But Vivian was clear when she said Aaron was moving on for now.

Vivian allowed Sarah to feel what Aaron was going through. Her choice was this life. His choice was Sarah. He had never been right with what she did, and having to chase her around and never know if she was alive or dead had taken its toll on him.

Sarah understood but didn't like it. She'd call him. They'd talk. She loved Aaron, and he loved her. But he was free to do as he wished. She would never hold him back.

It was time to let Aaron go.

Vivian whispered some of what was coming and why working alone was more important than ever. This time it wouldn't be so physical, so life and death for Sarah. Vivian dropped a few words and hints into Sarah's consciousness that put a mental picture together.

All Sarah had to do was find a certain number of people and change their plans. If their plans succeeded, it would mean the death of many.

It would be easy. Vivian would supply the locations and times. All Sarah had to do was convince them to stop going forward.

Sure, she had to convince them with a gun, but once convinced, everything would be fine, and Sarah's job would be complete.

Yeah, sounds easy, Vivian. Famous last words.

Do this and succeed, Vivian had whispered as Margot pulled into the hospital's parking lot, *or you will be unlucky.*

Who wants to be known as The Unlucky?

Sarah shuddered in her seat. As the word unlucky floated through her mind, she had a premonition of death, even torture. A feeling of being on the run like never before.

"What have you got planned, Sis?"

The car stopped in a spot.

"What was that?" Margot asked.

"Oh, nothing. Talking to myself."

"Right. Let's go visit the cop whose life you saved."

"Let's roll."

Sarah exited the car and followed Margot into the hospital, putting Vivian's thoughts away for now.

The images of what was next for Sarah were just too chilling.

Afterword

Welcome back to another segment in Sarah Robert's life. I hope you enjoyed the ride as Sarah found closure to a past that had haunted her for quite some time. Sarah's evolving, maturing still, her attitude calming, and her understanding of the world in relation to her gift developing in a way that allows her to do good in a world filled with bad. She's ready for *The Unlucky*, book thirteen, and many more to come.

I hadn't visited my brother's grave in over a decade. Now, before I get into trouble for that statement, let me explain. My brother is buried over four thousand miles from where I live. For the first time in nearly six years this summer, I found myself in Ontario, just east of Toronto, where he's buried, and I decided to make the jaunt over to pay my respects and leave flowers by his headstone.

My twelve-year-old daughter was with me when we found the graveyard and pulled into a strip mall across the street, intent on purchasing flowers. Neither store we visited had flowers for sale. Seriously unprepared, but at the cemetery already, my daughter and I decided to drive over and visit his grave anyway, sans flowers. (I know, how could I?).

As we headed to our car, a rented Ford Fusion, a raven fluttered from the lip of a garbage bin, startling both of us. When it did, a large bang emanated from inside the garbage bin, as if someone threw a chunk of metal inside, yet there was no one around, and nothing was tossed into it.

We looked at each other over the vehicle's roof, eyes wide, both thinking the same thing.

My dead brother just said hello. There was no explanation for the banging that resonated from the garbage bin.

Without debating beliefs, let me tell you that I believe in this sort of thing. Whether it truly was my brother or not doesn't really matter in the grand scheme of things. What matters to me is that I believe it was him, and he wanted us to know that he was there.

We got in the Ford, discussed what happened, and then headed over to the cemetery. Once parked by the mausoleum, my daughter and I ventured out to locate his gravestone. My brother's epitaph reads, *Life Goes On*, just like Vivian's.

Finally, as we headed back to the car, not five feet from the vehicle, the car alarm goes off. Now let me explain; there was no rational reason for this or any evidence to offer an explanation. The cemetery was virtually empty. No one bumped into the car. The keys were safely in my pocket.

There wasn't even a wind. Just the car alarm going off.

Again, my daughter and I eyed each other with a knowing stare.

I nodded, said a few words under my breath to my brother, and flicked the button to turn the alarm off.

After this experience, I had to write it in the first chapter with Aaron and Sarah at the cemetery. Sometimes not everything you read is fiction.

The name of the Amy Greg Psychiatric Hospital is entirely fiction. It's the hospital's name in my first novel, *Frequency of the Dead.* I miss that story and the Amy Greg facility, so I had to breathe a little life into it in this story.

Lastly, the receptionist, Sandra Gonzales, is named after one of my favorite readers. Sandra is an avid reader with a huge heart. She often sends me bits of wisdom and quips on writing and reading. Every time I hear from Sandra, I can't help but smile. If only the world could be filled with more Sandras, we'd all be better off. So, to Sandra Gonzales, thank you for being there and thank you for reading. May you continue your journey on this plane of existence for decades more, reading to your heart's content. And thank you for allowing me to name a character after you. God Bless.

And now off to write the finishing touches of *The Unlucky* so I can release it shortly after this one. There's a twist in *The Unlucky* that some of you might find unsettling, but hold on until the end and see how it all plays out. I hope you're still with me after that—or with Sarah, I mean.

Take care of yourself and your loved ones, and stay healthy.

Oh, and get caught reading.

I love you all,

Jonas Saul

About Jonas Saul

Jonas Saul is the bestselling author of the Sarah Roberts Series—more than two million sold!—and has written and published over sixty thrillers. After acquiring an agent, he signed several deals in Los Angeles, with MadRiver Pictures optioning his Sarah Roberts Series— over forty books!—(currently in development).

Jonas has often outranked Stephen King and Dean

Koontz on Amazon over the past decade. He's regularly invited to be a guest speaker, teacher, or workshop presenter at international writing conferences and film festivals worldwide. He hosts an annual writer's retreat in Greece, where he currently lives. He focuses his teaching on how to get tension and emotion in every scene, on every page, how he made it as a creator/writer, the path to success in this business, and the pitfalls to avoid. He also hosts a reading retreat in Greece with guest authors, yoga retreats, and hiking retreats. Visit the Imagine Greece Retreats website at www.imaginegreeceretreats.com, or email him directly to discuss an opportunity to join one of the retreats at jonas@imaginegreeceretreats.com.

Jonas is also a professional freelance editor. He works for several publishers and does private editing for clients, with many testimonials on his website at www.imaginepress.org, which details each author's response to Jonas's editing skills. Email Jonas directly for an editing quote at editor@imaginepress.org.

To book Jonas for a speaking engagement at a writer's conference/festival, to have him on your jury at a film festival, or even to say hello, email Jonas directly at jonassaul@icloud.com.

For updates on releases, hit the "Follow" button on Amazon or Bookbub, and join Jonas on Facebook, where he's most active.

Contact Jonas Saul

Linktree: Find me here

Email: jonassaul@icloud.com